LO FOR WORDS

G000093534

Amanda Addison

chipmunkapublishing
the mental health publisher
empowering people

Amanda Addison

Published by
Chipmunkapublishing
PO Box 6872
Brentwood
Essex CM13 1ZT
United Kingdom

http://www.chipmunkapublishing.com

Chipmunkapublishing gratefully acknowledges the support of Arts Council England.

'Language is the one thing that distinguishes us from other animals and... language is the most complex thing human beings do'
(Edward Saphir, 1921)

Amanda Addison

LOST FOR WORDS

Samantha picked up the faded book and held it close to her wet-suit. She changed into her stretch jeans revealing a red tattoo, which at a distance looked like a heart, but on closer inspection of her dimpled buttock was a carefully inked, single, red tulip. Still breathing heavily and spraying salt water from her strawberry blond hair onto the book, she ripped out several pages and stowed them under a folded deck chair. She peered around nervously as she padlocked the beach hut and set off across the sand for home.

Amanda Addison

LOST FOR WORDS

Chapter 1

If I look back, it all started that afternoon at The Upper Crust. As usual, Mum bleeped me a reminder on my mobile. I'm not crazy about that, yet I'm the most forgetful person you ever met in your life. I ran, dragging my portfolio through the fallen leaves into the back door of the bakery. The steam hit me like a plane door opening in Ibiza. I came face to face with Mrs. Plumb. I retched on the stale smell of her face powder which covered her warts; all five of them perched precariously on her double chin.

'What time do you call this?' she screeched looking up at the clock and almost dropping her tray of freshly creamed éclairs. Instead of her red face I saw Mrs. Punch, Queen of the Punch and Judy shows on Britannia pier. I stepped backwards, thinking that I would be banged on the head with the white plastic tray.

'I'll just get my overalls on,' I muttered to myself. Usually, she hardly ever listened to me when I said something. Not this time.

'Overalls! My employees don't wear no overalls,' she boomed, 'They're your baker's whites, Shaun. And don't forget you've got a five-tier wedding cake to finish. The Mavroudis were very specific about the sugar fishing boats,' she said in a voice becoming sweeter by the minute.

I wrestled to pull off my black jumper; for a moment I wished it didn't fit like a second skin and tied my hair into a pony tail, before she began her rant at teenagers: 'boys' hair today, you need a short back and sides.' I saw my reflection in the chrome ovens - white from head to toe. Let's say I never got on with uniforms - if I have to wear one I try to customize it. I can't tell you what I'd like to do with the white net cap which made me look like a girl. At least I still had my own boots on.

I simply thought of the money. Today's pay, cash in hand as always, and it would be my spending money for the college trip to Amsterdam.

I turned off the mixer and heard Mrs. Plumb, sliding white bloomer loaves into paper bags and prattling on to some old woman in the shop.

'That boy, I just can't have him out front again. He can't add up. Last Saturday the till was out by £5.93. And can I read his orders' list? He looks like he's listening. Then as soon as the customer's gone, he can't remember naught.'

It made me feel as small as the little wedding figures I would place on the cake. A shudder went down my spine; I always knew people said things like that about me. Different words come and go. When I was little I was remedial, then I had a statement. At high school I had a learning difficulty, now at art school, they said I have a learning difference. Whatever they called it made me feel depressed. Mum denied it all. She said I had a different view on the world, especially when I stop and start sentences and expect everyone to keep with my ideas. I knew the truth. I'm running to a different clock. I guess we all are, but I'm more out of step than most other people. That's probably why it took me so long to learn to tell the time. I don't wear a watch anyway. Not that I think watches are for the old, and those without a mobile. It's just they don't keep to my time.

'The state of education today,' Mrs. Plumb tutted and handed a bag of cream horns to the girl at the counter. I took off my cap and watched the girl from the kitchen doorway. Her skin was smooth and as richly coloured as the chocolate éclair icing; her dark hair peeked out from beneath her hippy head scarf.

'Don't get many like that round here - not yet,' muttered Mrs. Plumb under her breath. The girl wasn't even out of the door.

'Stop gawking,' yelled the Plumb bitch at me. 'Seen them down in London. You know. Darkies - Moslemists. We have to watch our backs, Shaun.'

It was hard to stand there and listen to that crap without saying anything. I didn't care what she thought. As I rolled out the last of the sugar boats I felt weightless, as if I'd grown wings and soared around through clouds of icing sugar. It was dark through the steamed up windows. I pushed the icing into the clay moulds I'd smuggled out of the 3D room at Gt Waveney School of Art.

Muffled voices leaked downstairs from Mrs. Plumb's television. It was safe to switch off the God-awful Radio Broadland and plug in my I-Pod. Prince William smiled down at me from the glossy poster. Apparently, he likes pop music too.

Iron Maiden pounded into me. I speeded up my rolling and hoped no one was watching as I waved the rolling pin around like a sword. A film of havoc; soldiers, rubble and tanks played behind my eyes. Don't get me wrong, I'm not into bombing innocent people, I'm just fascinated by it - how there's always been wars. Anyway, as I said I've got this phobia about uniforms, so I'd never make it in the army.

I like to make things whilst listening to music or doing something else, like watching the television. It helps me focus. They never believed this at school. I've got this idea that it's all because part of my brain is distracted leaving me free to invent.

The music slurred. There was a strangled noise like a wounded animal. Then nothing - silence. I pulled out the ear plugs. The white wires tangling with the fishing boats. A snow storm. A direct hit on the bakery.

As I spun around the kitchen I tripped into my art box, identical to Dad's black plastic fishing tackle box. It was then that I had an idea. I problem solve - but people never notice it. The clay modelling tools were perfect. The damaged boats now had hortpoles, I mean portholes, and wood textures, the lot!

There was a rumbling and some lights in the alleyway. It must be Mr. Plumb. *Why couldn't he be late - like he usually is?* I thought.

'You done lad,' said Mr. Plumb standing in the doorway. 'You look like you've stepped out of one of those snow storm shakers,' he laughed. Mr. Plumb gave me the creeps a bit, but I really liked him.

'Just a mouple of cinutes, I mean minutes,' I said, feeling embarrassed, as the words tumbled out back to front. I stared into the metal oven and brushed the icing sugar off my eyebrows. I arranged the last of the boats.

'Well done, Shaun. A good job,' said Mrs. Plumb, 'you certainly know your keel from your rudder, just like the rest of your family,' she said admiring the vast quantity of boats. The way I made them had nothing to do with knowing much about boats; I could see really clearly how all the parts went together. I could walk around it in my head before making it. Other people seemed really slow with things like that.

'I'm surprised any of my sponges rise these days. It's never been the same since we converted to North Sea gas,' she complained. 'Just a little extra from Dennis and me for your trip.'

'The minimum wage for a sixteen-year-old's not much is it? You've earnt your bonus,' said Dennis, slapping me on the shoulder.

'Spend it wisely!' she said, finally handing it to me. Several folded notes shone through the clear plastic packet.

'Plenty of Christmas cakes to ice when you get back!' said Mrs. Plumb licking a great dollop of icing off the palette knife. I really wanted to retch.

'Now help Den load up the van.' I knew the Mavroudis were a big family. Gt Waveney's Greek Mafia. The endless boxes of rolls and cakes were enough to feed the whole of Gt Waveney.

She climbed into the front of a white Fiorino, the cake box sat on her lap. She cradled it tightly like a baby,

'I'll just finish them off with a few pink chrysanths. Then we're done, Dennis. And 500% profit on these cakes,' she whispered, her eyes gleaming.

'Glynis. That lad will be the making of us,' he said.

'The next Jamie Oliver.'

'Not useless like our Jonathan. No sight or sound from him. Is London really that far away?' he lamented. Through the driver's mirror I watched him wipe his eyes. Mrs. Plumb was silenced for once. She looked straight ahead through the misty windscreen. 'What's that noise?' she shouted, as I crept out the back of the van.

She wound down the window, 'Now don't forget to wash those trays before you let yourself out.' The Plumbs screeched and reversed down the alleyway. Thank God they were gone! That little bit of eavesdropping in the van made me start to think they must be making mega bucks out of me. I didn't mind being used, as it made me feel for the first time ever, really good at something. I stacked the last of the white plastic trays onto the draining board. Then a funny thing happened; snap shots of the 'chocolate éclair' girl wouldn't leave my mind alone.

Chapter 2

The tide rushed in forming pools. My arms and legs carved a sand angel into the soft sand.

I felt a body heavy on top of me. I started joining images - her green eyes, which glowed brightly like the lights of the gas terminal; her black hair so smooth and glossy to touch, blew like a flag in the wind across the beach. Her scarf sparkled and bells tingled in my ears.

'Remember me,' said a soft, voice, almost a purr. Boom, boom roared the sea. I pulled her closer. You're probably wanting to know if it was a starry night and all that romantic stuff. I was enjoying being with her, everywhere else was blank and dark. I was in my room alone. Or so I thought.

'Picasso!' I shouted, as she dug her claw into my leg. A knock pounded on my bedroom door. The cat snuggled further under the duvet. I checked my mobile. The numbers glowed out: eleven-thirty.

'Come on Shaun. Wake up!' shouted Mum. 'You need to pack. How you slept through those gales I'll never know.'

'Not yet, the train isn't until this afternoon,' I groaned.

'It's your fault if you're tired. You shouldn't have taken that job. There's plenty of better jobs than that.' I don't know why she said that. She knew the fiasco I'd caused at 'The Pepper Pot Cafe' getting all the orders muddled and then charging the wrong prices. They'd said I had a lovely manner with the diners; one had called me charming, but they couldn't take the chaos and the losses. I only lasted a day.

Mum pushed hard, against the records, CDs and my washing which blocked the door.

'You let that cat sleep in your room again?'

'No!' I told her. Picasso, she's a girl by the way, wriggled out from the duvet and scuttled across the room. Mum rolled her eyes and started again.

'Something you need to do. Nan wants to see you before you go,' she said, winking. Then she threw a package onto the pile of clothes on top of the crumpled duvet.

'This is for you,' she said. 'I've been keeping it. Waiting for the right time.'

'Not another book Mum!' I said, feeling it through the plastic carrier bag. I don't get excited by books the way Mum does. I cringe to think how until a couple of years ago she had me carrying round plates of nibbles to her book club ladies, who exclaimed:

'What a sweet boy!' Those ladies weren't her friends anyway. They always said things like:

'Isn't it cozy here?' or, 'What a tight squeeze.' Most of them worked in the library and knew Mum well, for she borrowed one novel after another. Once I heard them discussing me,

'You need to foster a love of books in that boy. That'll get him over his reading problems.'

'Um,' was all Mum had said.

'Open this once you set sail. I'm going to put it in your bag now. And I want this room tidied up before you go,' she commanded.

I hid under my faux suede duvet cover. I didn't feel much like getting up. I knew where everything was in my room. What was the point of sorting it all out? Making it look neat and tidy. And just to please Mum. Dad was hardly there anyway. Now that he'd finally found a job. He worked three weeks off-shore, then two weeks off back in Gt Waveney, where he spent most of his days and often nights out fishing. He's a nice enough guy, used to take me to the park and amusements all the time. 'Get us both out of Mum's hair,' as he used to say. Now we don't have a whole lot in common.

The North Sea threw up a murky swirl of brown and grey, looking like something unmentionable from one of Nikki's toilet jokes. In the distance towards the horizon I glanced at the gas platform where Dad worked and turned in from the sea front and trod along Wellington Road. Nan's grubby stone clad bed and breakfast - *Belle Vue,* beckoned. I'm not too crazy about old buildings; they're all dark and gloomy. It was miles apart from the glass and chrome of contemporary architecture I had so enjoyed making models from at college. I rang on the bell and as always was surprised when it played God Save the Queen. The door opened and there stood the girl. The girl from my dream, **and** the girl from the bakery. The ring of the bell faded away and I heard my heart slam a quick pulse. Breathless, I stood on the step freeze-framed, as if in one of my animations.

'Hello, your Nan is out. It's her bingo afternoon. Your Nan, Mrs. Colby, was expecting you. She asked me to let you in,' said the girl, her dark hair falling onto her face. I swung round into the narrow hall-way. I looked long and hard at her almond shaped eyes rimmed in what looked like charcoal. Crash! Smash! I'd forgotten how big my backpack was. Before I knew it I'd collided with one of Nan's ornaments.

'Oh no! She'll go mad,' I exclaimed.

'She certainly spends a lot of time talking to them,' said the girl, raising her dark eye-brows. Yet who's to say she's mad?' Rows of long-lashed dolls stood to attention on the glass ledge which lined the length of the hallway. Their smooth, ivory complexions looked at me angrily. *She doesn't know Nan's little ways very well yet*, I thought to myself.

'Miss Jane, Miss Tilly, Miss Amanda..............,' she said. Then, holding the shattered doll in her hand, said, 'Look at Miss Mary.' I burst out laughing.

'You know when I was little I used to have nightmares about these. They'd come to life and walk up Nan's stairs and into the bedroom. I'd wake screaming, just as they stood over my bed.' I knew I was speaking really quickly by the look on her face. It was just that the words were tumbling over each other in their rush to get out of my head.

'Poor you! Anyway I haven't introduced myself properly. I'm Alice. Alice Nizami,' she smiled, tossing back her long hair, like some kind of model. Her crisp, clear voice wasn't local. It sounded more like a member of my Nan's and Mrs. Plumb's beloved Royal Family.

'I'll mend it before she gets back,' I said, looking down at one of the dolls I'd always hated.

'I promise you she'll never know what happened,' I said. I didn't tell Alice the truth, that if Nan knew I'd broken it she wouldn't give me any money for the trip. I slotted the pieces together, as speedy at assembling it as I was with Mum and Dad's flat pack furniture. My fingers slid across the pieces, which, like Nan's kitchen surfaces, were covered in a film of grease.

'So how come you're staying with Nan?' I ventured. 'Are you at the poultry factory, like all the others?' The moment I'd said it, I realised it was a stupid thing to say. It just came out before I'd thought about it. Even I could tell that she didn't act like any of Dad's old mates or sound like the migrant workers.

'No! No Way!' she exclaimed. 'Mrs. Colby is on the Art School's accommodation list. Apparently nobody comes here on holiday anymore.'

'Don't blame them,' I said.

'It's only temporary. I've just started at the Art School. I was a late applicant. I tried uni last year and let's say it wasn't for me,' she said, her face turning sad, almost ugly.

'I'm at the Art School too. Foundation course,' I added quickly.

'Yes, I know. Your Nan told me,' she said.

'So you've done A levels already?' I ventured, knowing that I couldn't leave school quick enough.

'Yeah. Not round here though,' she said, looking back down at the broken doll.

Alice held the porcelain in her long, thin hands whilst I squeezed on the super glue. It reminded me of the body casting we'd done that week. As usual Miklos wanted to show off his model body and I had to cover his torso with Vaseline before wrapping him in plaster bandages. I could see the top of her breasts peek over her striped jumper. If only I could have touched her, casted her and preserved her forever.

'A strange choice for your Nan!' exclaimed Alice, breaking my day-dream.

'That's Leonardo,' I said looking up at the picture of body organs and tracts.

'Yes, I know da Vinci's work,' she said in a hoity-toity way I didn't much like. What I had meant was, people in Gt Waveney don't know about Leonardo. And if they do, they don't **talk** about his pictures.

'Nan is always talking about her ailments.' I said, looking up from my puzzle. That was an understatement. It got on your nerves sometimes. She'd go on and on about herself, I was sorry for her, but I'd rather not hear it all. 'I bought if for her seventieth - I thought it might help her, to find out what's wrong with her. He, Leonardo was left-handed - like me. Look, you can see from the shading.'

'Yeah,' she said, unimpressed.

'And good at this too,' I said, passing her a piece of paper.

'Wow! How did you do that so quickly?' Alice looked down at her name written backwards, forwards and upside down.

'You can keep it if you like,' I offered, wanting to punch the air with my fist in triumph.

'Look, she's kept the cellophane on the frame!' she laughed, checking out her name in Nan's dirty mirror.

'As good as new,' I announced, slotting the last part of Miss Mary together. She seemed to like me. At least, I think she did. 'Fancy getting something to eat? I bet Nan won't be back for a while'.

Alice walked close to me, her patterned dress and striped jumper hung over her jeans. She looked great. I felt great, as if on some great adrenaline rush. I hoped everyone was looking at us. She was as dark as I am fair, or mousy and pasty by November, if I'm being honest. Her profile was elegant, her strong nose and chin made me hate my potato nose and round face. We passed pound shops full of fake jewellery and plastic gifts and I admired her reflections in their windows. I tried to keep the conversation going, pointing out all my childhood haunts. 'That's The World of Wax. I worked there at the end of year eleven – after my exams.' I didn't say that I only did two exams in the end: Art and Design Technology. Instead, I said, 'It's a rival to Madame Tussaud's in London, you know.' She didn't look very impressed, though. We reached the sea front and the water was almost blue now, mirroring the bright, bright sky.

Most places were boarded up for the winter. Even Aphrodite's Palace and The Pepper Pot were shut. I couldn't tell Alice how glad I was The Pepper Pot was shut, after that day in the summer I hadn't dared to walk past, yet alone go in. We were in luck. Through the steamed-up windows and grey nets there were lights on at the Sunrise Cafe.

'Come on,' I said. Alice grimaced. Inside it smelt just like Nan's kitchen. Alice stood very still and posed at the counter, she looked perfect, a bit like one of The World of Wax sculptures. It was decked in seaside postcards, of a summer that seemed so long ago.

'Two coffees and two of the cakes.'

'You mean the donuts, luv?' said the man.

'Yes, two donuts,' she said. She didn't seem to know what a donut was. I wasn't sure if I should pay. I'd asked her out, after all. Whilst I debated she handed over a tenner and then it was too late to offer. What I liked about her was how certain she was of everything.

We were the only customers in the silent cafe. How I wished the man would put the radio on. Even Radio Broadland would have been better than this silence. Silence made me feel buzzy, unable to operate. I needed some sound and I'd have felt much better, made a better impression with Alice. He watched us from behind his newspaper. I fiddled with the giant plastic tomatoes full of blood red ketchup.

'These are design icons now. Really hard to get hold of and worth a bit,' she said.

'They've never gone out of fashion here,' I said. She laughed. I bit into the sugary donut and bright red jam dribbled down my chin. Alice picked up a rough white serviette and wiped my chin clean.

'It's cochineal. Beetles' blood that makes it red,' I announced, remembering World of Wax factoids and unable to bear the quiet. She pushed her plate away and I felt a sinking sensation hit my stomach. I'd failed again. As usual I hadn't sorted out what I wanted to say; like the jam in the donut, it just gushed out whilst I was elsewhere.

The bells and flashing lights of the amusements lured me into the arcade. Alice watched me from the draughty entrance. I was caught in a loop, putting more and more money into the slot machines.

'Shaun, I'm going back now, I need to pack,' she said, yawning.

'Have you found a flat then? Somewhere more permanent?' I asked, barely glancing away from the bells and gold bars of the machine.

'No. I'm off on the trip to Amsterdam later. It's all happened so quickly. Starting at Art School. A cancellation on the trip. I didn't think I'd be off to Amsterdam at the end of my first week here. I need to get some new clothes.'

'You won't find anything in Gt Waveney. The shops around here are the real pits.' I shouted, unable to move from the machine.

'I thought as much. It's just full of chain stores. I want something a bit more individual. Anyway, nice to meet you,' she said, blowing a kiss as she left the arcade.

My wallet empty, I checked my messages. Nan! There were three from her.

'Hello, Bellevue, may I help you,' she answered in her best telephone voice. 'That you, Shaun?' she asked, 'Can't hear you over all those bells and beeps. So that's where you've been, down that arcade again. Forgot all about your old Nan? You coming round before you go?' she said, in her usual demanding voice. I sprinted round to Nelson Road.

'A kiss for your Nan!' she exclaimed, as I crossed the threshold. I obligingly pecked her on her cheek. Nan looked like one of those sad contestants on '*Not What To Wear*'; her stretch jeans hugged her wrinkled tan tights.

'Weren't busy for half term like we used to be. They've all gone to Spain for their hols. Can't complain. The contractors are better than nothing.'

'All right then, Nan?' I asked, hoping she'd say yes. But of course she didn't.

'Well, see as you're asking. The doctor still can't find nought wrong with me. With my bladder, my back, my eyes.' Uninvited, images of Alice's face invaded my head, and I couldn't switch them off. 'Are you listening, Shaun? Anyway, Dr Barnard says there's nothing more he can do for me. I'm a mystery. He's sending me to a specialist - a psychotherapist. I'm off there this afternoon as a matter of fact.' I forgot to tell you that I don't do doctors. At high school they wanted Mum to take me the GP. She'd flatly refused. She'd joked that Nan had used up our whole family's worth of healthcare.

'Nan, it's Saturday. Are you sure?' I said. It's not what you're thinking, Nan wasn't demented. She's always been in a kind of muddle. That's what Mum says - and it's why we can't move away from Gt Waveney. Although I overheard once, probably when Mum and Dad were arguing, that

Nan was told she was stupid and sent to some Goddamn awful school for backward children. Although in our family those sorts of things weren't ever openly discussed.

She brought out a letter from under a sea of papers.

'Look, oh I can't see the date. Must be my eyes. It was there last time I looked. Where's it gone?'

I slipped my finger down, carefully reading each line. I don't normally let people see me do that, but it didn't seem to matter with Nan. 'There it is Nan! Monday 7 November at 2.30. And it's to see a Doctor Merry.'

'Got a little something for your trip. Don't tell your mum,' said Nan changing the subject. 'She seems to be in a real state about you going off to Amsterdam. She's a fine one to talk, she was off here and there and out all night when she was your age.' *You've told me this a thousand times before*, I thought.

'Thanks Nan,' I said, stuffing a tenner into one of my many coat pockets.

'Now don't forget which pocket you've put it in. It was my lucky afternoon at the bingo. Off you go then. Get yourself ready,' said Nan edging me out into the street. 'You don't want to miss the boat,' she chuckled.

Chapter 3

'Shaun! Shaun! Great cakes,' called Miki and Nikki across the busy Wellington Road. I wished they'd seen me earlier with Alice by my side.

'Thanks, mate,' I said, feeling my face turning red, amidst the pale Saturday shoppers.

'Too good to eat, says Catarina,' Miki boomed.

'See you at the station,' yelled the twins in unison.

I watched them go into St Nicholas' church. The whole extended family was dressed in black. I'd never seen Miki and Nikki Mavroudis wear suits, yet alone posh black ones. Typically Nikki's buttons were almost popping off; whereas, Miki with his dark Greek eyes and curly black hair looked like a celebrity going to a film opening, all he needed was a red carpet. If there's one thing I hate it's guys who are vain. Little did I know then that pictures of him would be circulated around the world - but that comes later.

What I did feel envious of was their big, usually happy family. I'd never told anyone how much I hated being an only child. Somehow it would have made it worse, turned it into a problem if I'd admitted it. Most people have cousins and I didn't even have them. According to Nan we have lived on this stretch of coast for over 200 years. Yet, what remains of the Andersen and Colby families is so small we'd struggle to fill our living room with guests, yet alone an enormous church and the ballroom of the Hotel de Paris.

'Are you sure you've got everything?' said Dad as we drove past the docks. 'Look at those there ship names: *Achilles*, *Prinsengraacht*....' I wasn't interested in those foreign names. What I liked was the brightly coloured flags, ready to sail, and wave goodbye to Gt Waveney.

'When I was your age passengers could sail from here to Holland. It's a perfect horizontal line from here to Scheveningen,' said Dad.

'I guess no-one wants to come here these days,' I muttered.

'Plenty want to come here, Shaun,' he said, his voice rising. 'We're right on the edge of England, tipping into the sea. Gt Waveney is England's most Easterly point. In fact Granddad used to call it the German Sea.'

'Thanks for the geography lesson,' I muttered under my breath.

'Look at all those Portuguesers at the turkey factory,' Dad carried on, 'I was the last Englishman left standing on the production line. Even the health and safety signs were in Portuguese!'

'Good job you're on the rig, now, then?' I said, trying to avoid one of Dad's hard luck moments.

'Working as a roustabout, relentlessly scraping rust off the rig isn't exactly a good job. It brings in the dosh. I would have done it earlier, when you were growing up, but I didn't want to leave you just with your Mum and Nan when you were little,' he said. Dad had never talked like this before and I felt a bit uncomfortable and wondered what was coming next. Yet at that moment, to tell the truth I was more embarrassed by Dad's car.

Dad shut up and parked his old, silver Punto at Gt Waveney train station. I jumped out of the battered car. Why did he have to make matters worse and park it next to Tony Mavroudis' glossy black 4x4? Miki had made a quick change and was now dressed in jeans and soft black fitted coat. He stood against the car and looked like those black and white photos of George Clooney you see in glossy magazines, not that I'd be seen dead reading *Hello* or the like. Tony sat smugly in the car. Nikki banged on the window and shouted at him in Greek. He then resorted to gesturing madly in a sign language full of arm waving obscenities. I knew they were mad at each other, yet there was something really exciting about the way they behaved.

'They're discussing his wages at the kebaberie,' whispered Miki. 'Uncle Tony says he has to pay for what he eats out of his own wages,' he laughed. 'It's for his own good really,' he added, sounding as if he was talking about a kid brother rather than someone his own age.

'Hi Tony,' said Dad in his jovial way. Tony wound down the electric window and lifted an arm and waved back at us as if he were royalty.

'That Uncle of yours is a real success story of New Labour. He's a self-made business man,' said Dad. Miklos nodded. 'I remember when he first arrived from Cyprus with only eight pounds in his pocket. He's worked hard. And look at him now,' he added, glancing down at the black beast. Just then Tony revved up the engine, and with an unnecessary screech drove off into the sunset.

Dad escorted the three of us across the sad-looking car park towards the platform.

'You can go now,' I said, knowing how mean I sounded. I just thought *Dad may make some embarrassing goodbye scene in front of everyone.*

Dave and Tassy, the tutors, stood in front of the poky waiting room. They probably weren't used to the smell of cold concrete and pee. Tassy's rainbow-striped jumper brightened up the station. Mum had always asked me why all my art teachers had such appalling dress sense. I had mumbled something about individuality, not dressing from chain stores. I liked Tassy's clothes and wished Mum would dress a little more like her. Everyday Mum wears a pencil skirt and a shoulder-padded jacket. She's twenty years out of date. And she calls it good dress sense!

Dave ignored us. I thought it was just me that he ignored and probably didn't like. Am I paranoid? He was a bit old for a graphics tutor, he seemed more like a history teacher from high school. He was madly flapping sheets of paper, pens and paintbrushes. As usual, Tassy greeted me with a smile. Don't get me wrong, I didn't fancy her or anything, well maybe just a bit. I wasn't into the older woman thing - she must have been at least ten years older than us. It was more that I wished the world was more like Tassy. I wished home was more like Tassy.

'A make-do register,' she laughed. I signed my name on her scrap of paper. 'There should be thirteen of you. Anyone seen Alice Nazami?' she called.

'Alice who?' asked a couple of them.

'That half-caste girl,' whispered Lauren Jenks, stroking her mousy dread locks.

'She's not here,' said a boy, still staring at the engines and writing in his notebook.

'She's new. Only started this week,' replied Tassy. 'I haven't got an address or phone number. The train's in ten minutes,' she said, her voice becoming unusually shrill.

'She's living at my Nan's B & B,' I said. 'I could ring Nan if you like.'

'Oh could you? That would be brilliant,' smiled Tassy. I was only too glad to help. Of course Nikki and Miklos nudged and poked me.

I huddled in the corner of the station trying to get a signal.

'Shaun. What's up? Are you all right?' said Mum answering the phone.

'Oh, wrong number,' I said. 'I thought I'd rung Nan.'

'Have you got Nan's number?'

'Yes. I'm not stupid, Mum. I've got her number on my phone.'

'I didn't say you were stupid. Wait a minute. You did take the book didn't you?'

'Yes safe in my bag,' I said, not really sure or bothered if it was there or not.

'It's just that it is about us, our family.' Mum trailed off. I didn't have time for that and was about to key in Nan's number when,

'Shaun! Shaun!' shouted Tassy. I turned round and there stood Alice with the others by the train.

'Sorry. I'm terribly sorry. I haven't got a watch,' said Alice.

'Time you got one then,' joked Nikki. Alice didn't seem to find him funny.

Tassy stood engrossed in conversation with a balding, middle-aged man. I didn't really like the way he was looking at her.

'I'm the Mercury's chief reporter,' he said. But it wasn't him we noticed but the animated and good-looking young photographer, dressed in tatty jeans and soft, black leather jacket. The photographer shot about, flicking his dark glossy hair back as he arranged us. Bloody typical, he focused on Miklos and then moved Alice next to him, aiming for a shot which would be both glamorous and politically correct. It got on your nerves sometimes, how they always photographed the Mavroudis - the school prospectus, the council leaflet. I guess they were as dark as anyone got in Gt Waveney. To tell the truth it was only a couple of years ago that I first saw a black man in Gt Waveney. I think he was on holiday. Why should it matter what we look like?

'You're not from round here? Are you?' asked Nikki, standing awkwardly in front of the photographer. What's your name?' continued Nikki blocking his view. Nikki drove a lot of people crazy with his endless questioning. I liked him for it - in fact he often asked just what I was thinking, yet daren't in case people thought I was thick or something.

'Declan. Declan Cronin from Tooting,' answered the photographer, keen to get Nikki swiftly off his back.

'What are you doing up here, then?' continued Nikki unperturbed. This time the photographer blanked Nikki. He called to Dave in his thick cockney accent,

'Over 'ere mate! You're the art teacher aren't you?' Dave went pale, grabbed Tassy's arm and flung her into Declan's firing line.

'She's much prettier, more photogenic than me,' said Dave with a theatrical bow. The photographer now on a roll snapped away.'

'Thanks guys,' called Declan, 'Nice local story for the paper.'

The station house was at the end of the line, the last building before the marshes, from which the land spread out flat and thin like perfect pastry. Outsiders always said it looked like Holland, with its windmills and big skies - soon I'd know if they were right.

'Come on now, can't wait any longer,' called the conductor. I lugged Alice's heavy suitcase and my backpack onto the train.

With a whistle and a wave the train pulled out along the single track. The two-carriaged train, small and insignificant like my old toy railway, sped into the dusk, down to the port.

'Ah!' shouted Sophie. 'There's a bomb on board.'

'Bang! Bang! Scream! Another firework screamed out of the sky. The long line of bonfires lit up the shore and our route.

Chapter 4

I wrote my name in big round letters on the steamed up window. Through the letter 'S' shone Dunstowe station. The lights called out in the darkness, the only building visible for miles around.

'The last of England,' announced Alice. 'Look at that grand Victorian monstrosity - always showing off with their Roman pillars and arches.' I fidgeted a bit, unused to anyone talking like that and not sure what to say. 'Don't worry - I studied architectural history last year,' said Alice.

'Oh, really, that's cool,' I said, realising we might have something in common and not knowing quite how to keep the conversation going. My interest was in designing buildings, not ploughing through books and plans made by others. It began with my Lego creations and now my ideas were made from sugar icing - but one day I hoped my ideas would cease being models and become real, live buildings.

'It wasn't cool. I've had it with buildings,' she yawned. 'If all goes well this year, I want to become a painter.'

'This is it, folks,' announced Dave, pointing to stacks of brightly-coloured metal containers. Behind them was the ferry: the *Queen Beatrix* of the Netherlands.

Once on board the gigantic white beast, Tassy read out the cabin lists. We were assigned four to a cabin. (Oh I forgot to tell you how I have this awful urge to give machines animal or human traits. I don't normally tell people about it).

'Miki and Nikki, Shaun and Anthony, cabin three nine four.'

'Who's Anthony?' I whispered. Miki hunched his shoulders in reply. A small boy, wearing a green combat jumper and tight drain-pipe trousers, stepped forward.

'It's him - the train spotter,' muttered Miki.

The twins and Keith, his army surplus rucksack bobbing behind him, ran down the metal steps to check out their cabin. I lagged behind, waiting to hear which cabin would be Alice's. Time seemed to slow down. I loitered about, fiddled with putting a couple of things in and out of my rucksack. I began to run out of anything plausible to do.

'What are you waiting for, Shaun?' asked Dave. I ignored him and followed the others as slowly as I could down and down the steps into what looked like an underground maze. I felt like I was in the belly of the great white whale. I heard the water splashing about outside and soon the beast began to sway. There was no sign of the others.

I searched for my cabin. I remembered it was three something and knocked on the door of three two two.

'What's up?' said Tassy, opening her cabin door.

'Wrong door, sorry,' I said.

'Tassy, I'm ready,' I heard Alice's crisp, clear voice move closer.

'Hi!' Shaun,' she said. 'We're off to the bar. Going to check out the disco. Fancy coming along?'

I moved in front of my rucksack, unable to conceal its bulk and my good luck.

'Pop your bag in here,' offered Tassy calling my bluff.

The disco turned out to be even smaller than the cabins. In the corner of the bar, pinned to the floor, was a small scratched silver moon, the size of a doormat. It was framed by a couple of dim flashing lights. Dave sweated in his black leather jacket. A group of jovial lorry drivers surrounded him and competed with him in downing bottles of Amstel beer. I didn't like Dave. He was a fake. He never let on what he really thought. Listening to him was like watching a TV commercial.

'*Ninety-nine red balloons*,' shouted Dave excitedly, as if he were a disc jockey. 'I remember the original version of this.' The squat lorry driver, who sat very close beside him, nodded knowingly. There was a clattering sound by the steps as Nikki stumbled into the bar. He was followed by Miklos, sporting a black roll neck jumper.

'Where've you been?' they asked, smirking to look at Alice. Lauren Jenks followed them, dressed for the occasion in a crop top. It was so cropped that it revealed not only her pierced navel, but a tattoo of a butterfly just beneath her left breast. The lorry drivers' jaws dropped in unison. According to Dave, this time of year the drivers usually had the ferry to themselves.

The low, slow hum of the song of a reggae tune diffused across the dance floor. Nikki lunged at Lauren Jenks who willingly stopped and started across the dance floor, as the boat swayed, out of time to the music. It reminded me of our old school discos.

I asked Alice to order me a few Sambukas.

'Are you all right, Shaun?' asked Alice. 'You look rather green. The barman will be after me, supplying underage drinkers!' she said.

'I'm fine. Fine,' I remember saying.

'He's the slime green of Anthony's army jumper,' laughed Nikki.

'Clear off!' I slurred.

'Those your new jeans?' I asked Alice, touching her knee. A shock trickled through me, as if her knee were electric. Sex is something I just don't understand.

'My own design,' she said, admiring the bright floral inserts. I love colour. It took me all afternoon. You were right about Gt Waveney's shops. But brilliant charity shops. That's where I got the fabric. The fabric's like a sweet shop of shapes and colours.' The thought of sweets made my stomach turn. 'Shaun? What's up? You're not all right. Nikki's right, you do look just the colour of Anthony's jumper,' she said, almost laughing.

'I'm fine. Never felt better.' In many ways I had never felt better. I thought my chances with Alice were looking really good. Then it all turned sour. It was completely my own fault.

'I'm taking you back to your cabin,' commanded Alice.

We stumbled down to level two. The disco music thumped me in the stomach. I felt Alice's soft arm and pushed myself closer. As we edged around the corner, I shut my eyes and felt the boat, or was it me? spin round. I couldn't help myself. I think I managed to shoo Alice away before my cheese sandwiches and penguin bar exploded out onto the steps. I opened my eyes and saw the almost unrecognisable carefully packed tea which Mum had made.

'Your cabin's just down there,' pointed Alice, looking away from the vomit. I screwed up big time.

I tried the door - it was locked. I banged on the door. I threw my body at the door, just as Anthony's face peeped round the door. I went inside and fell into the bottom bunk. The last thing I heard was a knock at the door.

'This is Shaun's bag. Is he OK?' asked Alice. Without a word Anthony took the bag and slammed door shut. I couldn't move.

I was still flat on my back when I heard Anthony was snoring heavily above me. I switched on the bunk lamp and felt wide awake. I sat up, bumping my head on the top bunk,

'Bloody boat,' I snapped. There was a rustle from above and then silence. I took out the book Mum had packed and examined the hand-drawn cover of red and grey shapes. It looked like the 1980s record covers I'd flicked through on rainy Saturdays in Andy's Record Shop.

Samantha Colby's Diary

Wednesday September 11th 1985
I was up in the night again, desperate for a wee. Then at 7am I rushed into the loo, with my

transistor radio. I put it up full blast, U2's 'Gloria' and then the vomiting began........

'Mum! That's the pits,' I thought out loud, and slammed the book shut.

Footsteps got louder and louder along the corridor. In came the twins.

'Very contemporary,' sniggered Miki from the bathroom. I saw his reflection in the porthole window. He was admiring himself in the mirror. I played dead. I wasn't in the mood for mucking around with the twins.

'Kiki's kennel is bigger than this!' exclaimed Nikki, almost falling onto my backpack.

'Shaun's out like a log?' said Nikki.

'Best place for him,' snorted Miki. 'I think that new girl Alice has really got the hots for me. Don't you think?'

Chapter 5

A bang shuddered through the ferry. I sat bolt upright, banging my head against the top bunk again. On full alert, I thought of Al Quaeda and terror attacks. When I couldn't sleep at night I sometimes acted out stories where I was the hero. Like I said, I'd never join the military but I can't get rid of this image of me defending the lives of innocents, standing up for my beliefs. In my day life, I'd have to admit I usually run away from a fight. Yet this was no real terror attack. For one thing I was the only one awake. There was heavy snoring coming from all three of my shipmates. I felt my way in the dark to the porthole. All I could see was the black of a starless night. There was nothing to do but go back to bed and wrap myself up in the thin sheet and blanket and read. I flicked it open several pages into the text, hoping to avoid any further mention of sick.

Sam Colby's' Diary

In the cabin of the Floriade ferry, Mar 15th, 1985
I was early. She pointed to an up-turned plastic bucket. I squatted between the tulips, like pink and red lipsticks of Boots' make-up counter.

A cold wind blew across the square and through my leggings. I shuddered with the daffodil buds, which were closed tight, thinking it was still winter. The trader's voices dulled; there was a knocking and banging - closing time.

'It's time now,' she said; her fingerless gloves reached my eye-level.

I stared at her, shaking. The cow! There was no way out now. Especially after Dad dying....and Mum being carted off to hospital - again. I cleared my throat, holding back the tears. The flower lorry brightened up the empty market square; the sides were decorated like Mum's dinner plates, blue and white paintings of flowers, trees and windmills. The heavy doors clanked open. She pushed me into the giant refrigerator. The heavy door stood ajar; through the gap I saw him give her a tiny box, her eyes lit up as she opened it.

'A girl's best friend!' she exclaimed.

'You know, several hundred years ago I could have given you one of these,' said the man, holding up a red tulip. They cost the price of a house!'

'Well I never. The likes of me would have been rich,' she said looking at the tulip delivery. Well I've got my own fortune now,' she winked. 'A florist shop, or maybe a café where I could serve up cream teas and Black Forest gateau,' she said, licking her lips.

I shivered between the tulips and birds of paradise. Eventually the sway of the lorry ground to a halt. It was stationary for what seemed like ages. I checked my watch, the luminous digit glowed out – telling me that we'd only been travelling for an hour. Finally Mr. 'de Moye', as we all called him after the flower company, opened the doors and like fugitives we crept past the parked lorries and made our way to a cabin. I wrapped myself up in several blankets and finally stopped shivering. He told me to stay put and he'd bring some food later. He needn't have worried.

Jonathan's mum had insisted I take one of her prize winning Victoria sponges.

I felt tired. The letters and words floated around, taking on a life of their own.

This cabin is so tiny. I'd had visions of some kind of cruise liner. No such luck! Maybe Jonathan is right and I'm 'full of delusions of grandeur' as he says.

I'm looking out of my minuscule window, more like a telescope really. This is the reverse of a romantic sailing off into the sunset; we're leaving the orange sky and sailing into darkness.

At least Mum's being looked after, rather than sitting in a sea of bills, saying, 'I can't manage.' Although, I'm not sure what they're doing to her at Thorpe hospital. I'm also sick of everyone fussing round after her. It was always Dad who looked after me anyway. I still remember starting high school. You had to buy the fabric and make your own dress. The day before school started Dad came home with an old sewing machine he'd borrowed from someone at work and the special fabric from Palmers department store. We sat up to the early hours with Dad cutting out the fabric and me machining it together. Mum must have been in hospital then. What about me!

I rubbed my eyes. All of a sudden I started crying. I'd have given anything not to. At least the others were asleep. I surprised myself, as I felt my wet, clammy face. The words bounced around, stinging me like a ball. My hands trembling, I put the book down. The tears kept coming. I pushed my face into my pillow and hoped no one could hear me.

Chapter 6

A knock pounded at the cabin door.

'Disembarkation in thirty minutes,' called the steward. I felt as if I'd only just gone to sleep. *Where was everyone?* I threw on several T-shirts, one on top of the other. I glanced in the mirror and rather liked my unintentional layered look. I clanked up the empty metal stairs to the main deck.

'You're late.' The words came accusingly from the dark bar. I couldn't see Dave, lurking in the shadows. I was still trying to catch my breath and ignored Dave. I didn't feel like making excuses. The group pigged out on the freebie breakfast of bread, cheese and ham. The smell of the strong coffee, which looked like treacle, brought back memories of last night's overdose on Sambuka.

'You were dead to the world,' said Nikki. 'We couldn't wake you, even when Miki sat on you!' I joined in laughing at myself and grabbed a crusty roll and cheese off Nikki's plate and downed it in one. 'A bit of ham,' said Nikki, holding it up to my nose. 'Oh sorry, I forgot you were veggie,' he added.

'Land ahoy!' called Anthony running over with his binoculars hanging round his neck. Like a sheep I followed the others over to the window and saw in the early morning light.

'Look! Scheveningen,' announced Tassy.

'Schevy what? It all sounds double Dutch to me,' laughed Nikki.

We slowed down, as if the big beast had run out of steam and had to crawl into the harbour.

'Its long sandy beach mirrors Gt Waveney's own Golden Mile,' said Tassy.

'It's the same latitude as Gt Waveney,' Anthony informed us all.

'Same lati -what?' giggled Lauren Jenks.

'It's a perfect horizontal line from Gt Waveney to here,' he explained to anyone who would listen as he gazed at his own map of England and Holland.

'Where's the boarded up shops and houses?' asked Nikki, enthusiastically. I loved Scheveningen at first sight. I gazed at the glass arcades and futuristic buildings. *Why couldn't Gt Waveney be like this?* I thought.

'One day I'll design something like that.' I confided to Alice. I starred into a space beyond the marram grasses and thick sandy beach. *What the hell had Mum been doing in Amsterdam? She never went anywhere.*

'You look miles away. Are you feeling all right now?' whispered Alice. I smiled my cheeky grin at her. I thought I'd be feeling much, much better by then. What am I doing thinking about Mum when I might have my first girlfriend, I thought. 'The diary!' I shouted.

I sprinted to the cabin deck. A boy, probably the same age as me, but immaculate in his black and white uniform patrolled the corridor with a giant plastic bag. Through the clear bin bag amongst Nikki's sweet wrappers and beer bottles - there it was - the diary. I followed him for a bit, feeling too cowardly to ask him if I could look inside. Then over the tannoy came an announcement; it was Dave.

'Could Shaun Andersen please join his party up on deck four adjacent to the entrance to the gift shop?' I lost my reserve and through a bit of sign language and shouting I found the book. It turned out quite embarrassing because he turned round and answered me in perfect English after I'd done some God-awful charade mime of reading a book.

I could hardly breathe by the time I reached the gift shop. 'You should have seen Dave, he practically fought to use the tannoy system, pushing the purser out of the way,' said Lauren, relishing the gossip.

I'd never been on a tram before. Nor had Miki; it almost caught his Greek sculptured nose in the quick shutting door. It was the first time I saw Alice laugh, the corners of her mouth arched in a lopsided grin. And the joke was on Miki; one nil to me I thought. We rattled along, sandwiched between perfectly straight dikes. It looked so like the stretch between Gt Waveney and Norwich. Smartly-dressed suits carrying briefcases joined us from the old fashioned villas, and rubbed their tall shoulders with us bleary-eyed students.

From The Hague we boarded a double-decker train bound for Amsterdam. We all made for the upstairs and sped through fields even flatter than Norfolk. We stopped at towns as square and straight as anyone could imagine. They were like my childhood sketches of fantasy cities.

'Sketchbooks out,' enthused Dave. 'An architect's vision of Mondrian's painted lines and geometric shapes,' he said, stroking his mousy beard.

'What, what sir?' asked a baffled Nikki. I never really knew why Nikki had gone to the art school. He's a nice enough guy but he never sees things. He always does just enough work but it's so dull. I swear he's only there because Miki is. Come to think of it he's always in Miki's shadow. I hate it how Miki basks in the spotlight, always getting attention.

'It's Dave. Not sir. How many times do I have to tell you you're not at high school now,' he snapped at Nikki.

'You weren't the only one who had too much to drink last night,' whispered Nikki to me, with one eye fixed on Dave.

'Just draw what you see. Don't worry about the train moving,' said Dave. Nikki huffed and puffed, did as he was told and filled his sketchbook with scribbles.

'I can't draw now! The train is moving. This is stupid!' he exclaimed.

The train edged into Amsterdam Central Station. I stuck with the others, as we crossed the station concourse. Lauren Jenks brought up the rear, barely walking in her tall, pointed black boots.

'Bit different to Gt Waveney!' exclaimed Dave. Of course it was different to Gt Waveney. I felt alive. Really alive. It was as though until then I'd been living in a grey fog that was home.

Chapter 7

I lugged mine and Alice's bags into the reception of the Hans Brenker hostel. I hoped it would earn me some points after I'd practically vomited over her designer jeans last night. I loved the bright graffiti-like murals which covered the walls. The giant squares, circles and hexagons outlined in black, shone like stained glass. It was like we'd left one of those old black and white movies, which was home, and walked into a world of full colour.

'You all need to hand in your passports, sign in, collect your dorm keys, drop your stuff off and get back to reception - pronto,' commanded Dave, taking off his jacket to reveal a bright Hawaii shirt covered in palm trees. He'd become increasingly tense and bossy. A vision flicked through my mind of Dave holding a police megaphone, keeping us criminals - or should I say students - in line. Even Tassy side-lined him and stood with us -the students.

'Should we let them have our passports?' asked Lauren, holding up her brand new passport.

'It's just a formality, Lauren. Nothing to worry about,' said Tassy.

It was then I remembered Mum saying the same thing at the apartment block in Ibiza. Everyone had laughed at her - even Dad, although he'd have probably said it if Mum hadn't. It was our first family holiday abroad, partly in celebration of Dad getting the job on the rig.

'The shape of things to come,' he'd said. Now we seemed to do very little together, since

Dad spent all his wages on fishing gear. 'How many rods and waders does a man need?' Mum had said. It was Mum's first passport. There'd been a real fuss trying to find her birth certificate in Nan's boxes and boxes of unfiled papers. *So how did she go to Amsterdam all those years ago? It didn't make sense. Moreover, why did she go?*

'Come on Shaun. Keep up,' said Dave prodding me in my kidneys.

'He'll have you for assault,' joked Nikki. Dave didn't laugh. We let out our collective moan and headed up the staircase. Our grey and black clothes circled round the landing. We looked dull and subdued against the brightly painted walls.

'Take one and pass it on,' said Dave. 'Just look at these glossy, bright Dutch graphics,' he said, excitedly flapping several of the maps high in the air. 'They are a work of art in themselves. Feel this,' he said, lovingly stroking them. 'The designers have even considered the paper. Just the right thickness. Not too shiny, not too rough.'

Nikki stroked his map as if it was a girl and a roar went out.

'Rumour has it, he's a failed graphic designer,' mumbled Miki against the laughter.

'Central Station seems to act as a focal point, rather like the effect of throwing a pebble in a pond from which concentric canals ripple out,' continued Dave, oblivious to Nikki's mime art.

'He's still drunk!' I whispered to Alice, her sweet perfume smelt exotic, just like my incense sticks I hid in my bedroom at home. So close to her I felt my whole body tingle. I couldn't listen to any more of Dave's ramblings for the whole world seemed to have opened out with possibilities. He went on and on.

'This is a truly inspirational city.' For a moment he seemed to lose his concentration, and then continued. 'Today we're starting with a walk down to the Dam Square, then the Van Gogh Museum. Oh! Van Gogh. What a man! What an artist!'

Alice turned and smiled at me. Nkiki saw, and of course nudged me in his stupid, childish way.

'You scored there, mate.

'Plus to finish us all off,' Dave sniggered. 'An early evening stroll to the red light area.' Suddenly we woke from our dream. 'Thought that would get your attention,' he said. I looked at Alice, expecting her to laugh. She didn't. I saw that ugly contorted face, a bit like a Francis Bacon painting if you know his work. He makes people look like angry slabs of flesh. *What was it with Alice? Would I have to tread on egg shells? Was she really so prim and proper and grown up. Was she a virgin?*

We stepped outside. The fresh clear air hit me after the overheated hostel. We passed tall, looming canal houses with enormous sparkling windows. Each building looked down on its mirror image in the brown canal water. Occasionally the perfect reflections were broken up by the odd dead bird or submerged, rusty bicycle. I knew I really liked this place already. You might think a few hours aren't enough to go on. But I decided then and there; after my foundation course I'm leaving Gt Waveney. We marched onwards,

Lauren Jenks and her new found mate, Nikki Mavroudis, drifted further and further behind. We became a disjointed crocodile. Rixy didn't look at anything. He kept his head down holding his map against his chest like a teddy bear.

Alice stopped and started looking at whatever took her fancy. She seemed to have her own ideas, which didn't include following Dave's orders. We passed tacky, neon-lit shops and bars; I must admit they did resemble Gt Waveney's Golden Mile, just a bit. Their signs dim, unable to compete with the harsh, clear light of day. Finally, we reached Dam Square. We stopped and huddled around Tassy.

'Where are Lauren and Nikki?' asked Tassy, her voice sounding stressed. Like a many-headed freak we all turned at the very same moment towards the direction from which we'd come. And there were a smiling Lauren and a grinning Nikki, in deep conversation as they crossed the road.

Look out! You dozy idiots,' shouted Anthony Rix, the spokesman for the many-eyed monster, in the direction of the happy couple. Nikki tugged on Lauren's bare midriff. Lauren, stood, mouth ajar as she watched the bicycle, with a wicker basket full of groceries and a dozing cat miss her by inches. Alice looked at me again, a kind of knowing look.

'The Dam has acted as the heart of the city since the first Dam was built here across the Amstel in 1270.' Dave pointed to the Royal Palace and the New Church. Nikki yawned. Lauren stuck out her tongue and revealed three silver nuggets. Rixy stood next to me and kept his head down in his map. It was hard to see what he was getting out of the trip, but I kind of liked the way he did his own thing whilst Dave thought he was being a model student.

'In the 1960s, this was the centre of all things hippy and psychedelic,' interjected Dave, as the group stopped fidgeting and became interested in its more recent history. 'You should have seen it then, people camped out here. Living from day to day, just for the music......um...they say Bob Dylan was even here.' Miklos, fed up with Daves's ramblings, looked him in the eye and asked:

'So, were you actually here in the sixties?' his dark eyes stared him out.

'Well, er, no, not exactly. Too young you see,' he chortled. 'Time to get some work done now,' he said.

Too tired to argue, we obediently took out our sketchbooks. Some, like Rixy, settled down quickly, and drew whatever happened to be in front of them - when Dave walked past. Once he'd gone past him out came the map. Alice looked up at the Nieuwe Kerk and the adjacent buildings and began to draw. It was like magic, the building coming to life on the paper.

'Not only are the buildings enormous, some also seem to be tilting like the leaning tower of Pisa,' she said, looking up at me. 'I guess it's the subsidence, all that damp,' she said. Girls I'd met before didn't talk that way. I was desperate to say something clever, well, funny really. Yet when I looked at the several false starts in her sketchbook they looked child-like.

'I never really understood perspective,' she said. 'My drawings are all about colour and my imagination.'

'How do you do that?' she asked. I shrugged my shoulders.

'I've always drawn. I could draw before I could write,' I said. What I really wanted to say was that as a kid I'd had to find a different way of saying things. I thought in pictures.

'It's just buildings aren't really my thing,' she said, laughing.

It made me think back to primary school; a shudder went down my spine. I wasn't joking when I said I could draw before I could write. I still couldn't write very well. I could hear Mrs. Jones' shrill voice:

'You're just not trying are you Shaun? You belligerent boy! You're just thick. You'll never get anywhere.' Well, she didn't see Jaime Oliver on telly. I know that's an enormous leap - that's exactly what Mrs. Jones didn't like or get about me, but I'll get to the Jaime Oliver connection in a moment. Like me, Jaime was in the remedial group, and now look at him; I wanted to tell Mrs. Jones. After that programme I'd seen the vacancy sign at The Upper Crust and passed Mrs. Plumb's sugar craft test. My first great exam success.

I half noticed the others packing sketchbooks away and standing up. They were off again! The world always seemed ahead of me. I carried on. I sometimes think that I literally travel to another place when I'm drawing. The world outside of me and my drawing is like a hazy background to where the real action is, me drawing. I'm not religious or anything like Miki and Nikki, always off college for one festival after another, but when I'm drawing or making, my head's gone somewhere and unravelled, the usual muddle. I heard the others, but it was if they were on television, not real.

'Time to go to the market. You must all be starving,' said Tassy, who keenly walked on.

'Haven't finished my barge,' said Nikki.

'Shouldn't take so long to get started,' smirked Lauren Jenks.

'You'll have to use your imagination and finish it later, or take a photo,' said Dave.

'You said not to work from photos,' Nikki replied. Dave didn't answer.

'Ouch!' Nikki slapped me on the back. I jumped up and we began mucking about. Just play fighting.

'God sake, boys! You're not on the playground now,' moaned Dave.

Nikki and I slapped each other on the back, and jumped in the tram to the Albert Cuyp market. The long narrow street continued into the horizon. 'This is the most famous market in Amsterdam. There's time for lunch and shopping. Meet back here at two o' clock sharp,' Tassy reminded us.

I spotted Alice, alone, leaning against a wall scribbling furiously onto the back of a post card. She looked up, startled.

'What are you doing?' I asked, making her jump as I peered over her shoulder

'Just some ideas. Sometimes it's easier to write than draw,' confessed Alice. 'Don't you?'

'Well, no,' I said, truthfully, 'that's why I'm at the Art School.'

'There's nowhere to hide. Is there? From the group, I mean,' she said, stuffing the postcards back into a paper bag. 'Let's go eat,' she announced.

Alice and I headed for the chip stall and warmed up on the piping hot chips, just as I did most lunchtimes in Gt Waveney, first at High School and now at the Art School. Some things never change, I thought. Except in Amsterdam it was better. They were served with generous dollops of creamy mayonnaise. Lauren, her dreadlocks flapping in the wind, sidled up to us. She was laden down with brightly coloured carrier bags.

'Let's see what you've got then,' I said, trying to sound interested for Alice's sake. Lauren pulled out a black roll neck jumper and a black and white check Crimplene mini-skirt.

'Real sixties stuff. Vintage fashion,' she said proudly. Nikki had now joined us. He admired Lauren's purchases, as if they somehow meant she was improved because she could buy clothes. He picked up a pickled herring and let it slither down his throat.

'You're revolting, Nikki! What are they anyway?' asked Lauren.

'Live herrings. Want one, Lauren?'

'Ah!' screamed Lauren.

'Stop it, Nikki!' commanded Alice. 'Don't worry, Lauren. They're not live, just raw.'

'Shauny,' whined Lauren, 'thing is I've spent all my money. And as we were at school together and everything. I'm starving. I was just wondering...'

51

'You've been ripped off!' exclaimed Alice. 'Haven't you ever been to Camden market? You'd get that lot for half the price.'

'Camden market? Where's that?'

'London,' said Alice, rolling her dark eyes.

'I've never been to London,' she said. 'What's more I'm hungry,' said Lauren, sounding like a whingeing brat. We all knew Lauren was a freeloader. Not that I'd say that to her face. We all just have our excuses ready. I, for one was about to say I hadn't got any change. Alice handed Lauren a bundle of Euros.

'You didn't need to do that' I said, watching Lauren join the chip queue.

'It's only money,' shrugged Alice.

Chapter 8

Our broken crocodile weaved its way through the cold damp to the entrance. I couldn't understand why on earth Nikki and Lauren were still holding out their phones taking photos of everyone; for we all looked tired and red-eyed like some awful flash photo. I'd switched my phone off after talking to Mum at the train station. I wanted a break with home and didn't even want to check my messages.

'Hurrah!' everyone cheered, when Dave emerged with a long reel of tickets for the Van Gogh Museum. I didn't cheer and am going to sound a bit of a geek now, but I enjoyed the chance to look at the building. Rietveld designed it. Most people won't have heard of him, but I think it's him that's inspired all the latest buildings in Gt Waveney and up in Norwich. We've been refrigerated, no what I mean is regenerated with lots of lottery money. He's become a hero of mine.

The museum is clean-lined and bright with lots of glass and stone floors. Hey, I'm sounding like an art history tutor. But standing there in the queue when we'd all run out of anything to say to each other I remembered something really strange. I was a kid, five or six and staying with Mum at Nan's house. I'd picked up her swirly gold tray and wandered around the house collecting up all her ornaments; the porcelain dolls, mugs with pictures of the royal family, miniature pottery animals, the lot. I'd walked into the kitchen and both Mum and Nan stood with a look of horror. Years later Mum told me that she hadn't been worried about a five year old thinking the house was a tip, it was more what Nan would do if I dropped them. 'Shaun. Don't move!' Mum had shouted, as if I were carrying a gun. She slowly walked over to me and took the tray, as if it were a baby I was holding for ransom. Nan one ever mentioned it again.

Something else happened at the museum, which I didn't really get at first. I never guessed that Alice was trying to tell me something important about herself with the episode in the Van Gogh Museum. We rode up in the glass lift and stepped into the galleries. I felt the floor sway as if still on the boat. The pictures came in and blurred out of focus, as if I were seeing them through a zoom lens.

'Have a wander round. Get the feel of the place, just see what appeals to you,' said Tassy in that kind voice of hers.

'And do split up. Some of you look like you're stuck together with PVA glue,' said Dave glaring at Lauren and Nikki.

The others disappeared into the brightness of the gallery. I wandered round in a kind of daze, unable to settle, unable to take in any of the pictures. I've always found galleries a bit like that. Too much of a sensory overload is the correct term. Not that I've been to many galleries. The Van Gogh Museum was the second one I've ever visited. We took a day trip to the Tate when I was at high school. The old power-station-turned-gallery was the biggest building I'd ever been to. In that space I felt as if I wanted to run through the building, past the giant spider and shout something out, although I'm not sure what I would have told the world. Of course I didn't do that. I sat, sweating in my polyester uniform and answered the questions on my clip board. So no one ever knew how excited I felt. Us, I mean teenagers are brilliant at fooling the world. They like it when we sit quietly and tick and fill in the boxes. It was my first trip to London **and** to a gallery.

It was when I was dithering about where to go that I spotted Alice huddled in the corner, making a really odd gulping noise, a bit like an animal. My instinct was to walk away, to think it was one of those girl things, crying one minute, on top of the world the next. I knew it was the selfish part of me, out to make a good impression, which stood there looking down onto her glossy black hair.

I hovered there for some time before she looked up, her face red and blotchy. I stared into her watery eyes; dark pools stared back at me. They held my stare. Self-conscious as usual, I was the first to look away.

I should have paid more attention to the Van Gogh painting in front of her. But then I had no idea that a painting could reduce someone to tears. He, Van Gogh that is, sat smoking a pipe. His cool blue eyes starred out as unrelenting as Alice's had been. Behind him, 'raged a hot, burning swirl of orange', Alice's words, not mine. 'Why do you think he did it?' she asked.

'Did what?' I answered. She pointed to her ear. What I failed to notice, were the white bandages wrapped round his ear like a bow on a Victorian bonnet. 'Oh that. Who in their right mind would do that?' I said thinking of Nan and the stories of Granddad forever finding her on the beach in her night gown and taking her home. Nan hadn't done anything like that in my life time, thank God.

I crouched down next to Alice. I ferreted about searching several pockets for a tissue. Eventually I handed her a crumpled tissue. She looked at it and laughed.

'Shaun, you're such a sweet guy. But that hanky is disgusting.' We both laughed. She pressed her hand down on me and stood up. I felt the strangest sensation, as like an electric shock when you touch the escalator in Palmer's department store.

'I'm going up to the study centre,' she said. 'There are piles of letters he wrote. I have to see them.' *Was she trying to avoid me?* Girls always rushed off just as things looked like they're going ok.

'I'll stay with the paintings,' I said, not really playing hard to get. But who on earth wants to read Van Gogh's letters when you've got the paintings in front of you, I thought.

The next time I caught up with Alice was after the gallery. In the end I'd gone up to look for her, but there was no sign of Alice anywhere. We were off on the march again. Dave led us like some military campaign, ready to conquer the city. The tall buildings cast cold shadows of an early twilight. Alice strode ahead, keeping up with Tassy's fast pace. I strained to hear their conversation.

'Why are you wearing that white flower?' Alice asked.

'It's a peace poppy,' said Tassy.

'Disgusting! Should be wearing a red one, like everyone else,' said Anthony in his usual monotone. 'My great Granddad had his thumb shot off in the war.' For a moment Alice's face turned a steely grey and I really thought she was going to hit him. And then, in a split second she was back to normal - her beautiful self.

Immediately all our moods changed. Maybe it was because it was suddenly dark, like stepping from one scene into the next. I felt a shiver go down my spine. I didn't think it would be like that. I thought it'd be like going to the Pleasure Beach at home. Nikki stopped nudging me. Even Lauren ceased her endless gossip.

Dave hadn't been joking about the red light district. It was as if we passed through an invisible border; from little book shop windows lined with books old and new, antique shops displaying heavy wooden furniture stood beside a hand-made chocolate shop. I studied the chocolate creations, the beautiful papers and ribbons and thought how Mrs. Plumb's grubby net curtained window display could be improved. These turned into shop windows of people.

A dusky-skinned woman sat in the window, her bare, voluminous, unnatural breasts bobbed between lengths of ivory knitting. They swayed like some exotic fruit. Even Pam, our life model at college, wasn't that big!

'Look at her Miss. Isn't she gorgeous?' said Nikki, his voice breaking the ice. His brown eyes bulged like a frog. Lauren glared at him. I think she was also mesmerized by the silky-limbed woman. She began to dance. Yet it was more like telly, watching her shielded behind a pane of glass.

'Nikki, I'm sorry to disappoint you. But she is a he,' said Tassy. Lauren hooted one of her fake laughs.

'But how do you know?' his voice trailed off. I'd never seen Nikki's olive skin blush, but I swear it did then.

I could just about make out Dave in the distance. He was making odd arm signals, as if he were some traffic warden. Eventually some of the 'keenies' from the group wandered over amidst the rush hour of trams, cyclists and pedestrians. I'd had enough of Dave thinking he could boss us about like a group of school kids and sat down with my sketchbook. I rather liked capturing everyone rushing here and there; their expressions some like stunned animals, others so blank I wondered what went on behind their mask.

I don't know how long I sat there, but when I glanced up I thought I saw a tram door close on Tassy and the others. I'm also sure I saw Dave vanish into the crowds, alone. I carried on sketching. It's hard to describe but I got absorbed in it, like entering another world, almost the same as when I'm playing computer games, except I have a picture at the end. I don't know how long I carried on for, but when I stood up I had to jump up and down to stop my pins and needles. The street had emptied out of day trippers. And I was alone.

Chapter 9

I walked all the way back to the hostel. It began to drizzle and I stuffed my sketchbook inside my coat. My sketchbook was all that I had left. I guess I should fill you in on the bit in between, tell you how I'd spent all my money and lost my phone. The evening's events rattled through my head. It was like a roller coaster ride down at the pleasure beach; once I got on there was no escape; I just kept going until it stopped. At least that's the version of events I kept telling myself.

It began when a tall, bony guy, it was as if I could see his skull through his thin face, beckoned me over. He looked friendly enough, although a little weird. I thought he wanted to know the time, or something. That was my first mistake. I should have just ignored him.

'I'll offer you a special discount. It's Happy Hour,' he said. I knew all about Happy Hours; Nikki and I spent the first afternoon after college at an end of season Happy Hour on the front. We'd drunk two for the price of one until we'd stumbled home at 7 o'clock. Dad had said, 'See what you get for your education - layabout students. And art students are the worst!' I didn't know if he'd been joking and I'm still not sure.

Anyway, I was cold and still pretty numb after sitting still for so long, so I went inside. My guts were still reeling a bit from the Sambuka, but a shot of whisky or brandy might warm me up, I thought. Not that I'd ever tried whisky or brandy, it was just that Nan always said, 'a drop of brandy warms the cockles of my heart.'

'What will you have? Now let me guess,' said the tall guy.

'A whisky or brandy will be just fine,' I said. 'I need warming up.' He let out an enormous roar, and then beckoned me in. Once I was over the threshold, there was no going back. It was like the Dracula story, for he might as well have said 'enter freely', for then there seemed no way out.

He handed me a clear looking drink, I knew from the colour it wasn't brandy or whisky. I sniffed it; it smelt of berries and Nan.

'Best Dutch gin!' he said pouring himself a glass and downing it in one. 'Now getting back to my question. Fair, dark, very dark, tall, short, you name it, I've got it. Quiet time of night, quiet time of year.' Suddenly, it dawned on me that he wasn't talking about drinks - but girls. I felt my face redden. In as deep a voice as possible, I said: 'Dark hair and brown eyes. Sort of exotic looking.' In my mind I had a picture of Alice and continued to describe it.

'Opposites attract,' said the man through his crooked teeth. I hadn't thought of it that way, but I was certainly bored with my own pale, pasty complexion and fair hair.

'Maybe more Middle Eastern than oriental,' I added, getting into the swing of things.

'It's not a candy shop, mate.' The guy said, before nudging me in the chest.

The next thing I remember is being in a back room. The damp walls had the earthy smell of the canals. The girl came in and took her dress off right away and chucked it on the futon. She had a black bra and lacy pants. She sat down and kept crossing and uncrossing her legs. She seemed really nervous for a prostitute and offered me a spliff.

'Sorry I don't smoke,' I said, immediately wishing I'd taken it, as I felt the spotlight was on me not her. She had a sort of deep voice which didn't go at all with her little skinny body. She looked at the clock, got up and took her bra and pants off.

You might think it was every sixteen-year-old's dream, but I didn't feel sexy at all. My stomach twisted like knots. And instead of anticipating my first proper (for all the gropes and snogs with Lauren at school didn't mean much) sexual experience, I felt like I was back in the life drawing room. But unlike the life drawing room, where the models were bored housewives called Pam or Bev, who insisted on wearing a bikini; or the man called Brian, whose head was decidedly out of proportion, this girl was different to them; she was beautiful. There was something about the way she moved, the tilt of her head and the slightly sad expression on her face which reminded me of Alice.

'What's your name,' I asked.

'Let's get going, honey,' she said.

'Could you sit like this for a few minutes,' I said, arranging her into a reclining position on the futon. I felt a bit bad. But unlike Alice, she was a real live girl and maybe Alice was only the girl of my dreams. Or maybe I'm just making excuses for what happened next.

The girl stared vacantly ahead, her features not quite European, not quite Oriental. The guy with the bad teeth had made a good choice, although she was a lacking some nice curves. I drew sweeping lines out from the centre of the blank page, the scratching of the pencil amplified in the tall, empty room. I came to an abrupt standstill and looked up from my drawing. It was good. One of those rare drawings when everything comes together and you feel it wasn't really you who'd drawn it, but some guiding hand. I was on a roll and ready for the next pose. If only I had some paints, I thought. Then, like Gauguin's women of the South Sea islands, I could have painted her in rich browns and golds.

I walked over to the girl and began to arrange her into another position.

'Like that, leaning.' I said. She pulled me down on top of her and that was the end of my drawing.

The whole experience hadn't been quite as I'd imagined it. Each scene felt unreal as though I were watching someone else, but my sketchbook was evidence enough that I had been there and something with a naked girl had happened. The sea of damaged, wild faces on the streets made me shudder. I thought of the bulging eyes in the paintings at the Van Gogh museum. Drenched in a blanket of cold fog I felt lonely and rotten. It was depressing out on the streets, yet I felt camaraderie with Van Gogh, he'd befriended a prostitute, he'd been broke.

Chapter 10
Samantha's story, the night Shaun left for Holland

God, what a day. Samantha munched on the fat chips and slouched on the leather sofa. The ice dancing wannabes blasted out from the television. A small portion of chips wouldn't do her any harm. Would they? After all, she'd swum her mile along the coast. Every day, whatever the weather she'd swum in the sea for the last twenty years. At first it had been a new beginning. It usually did the trick of straightening out her mind. Today she'd swum for a bit and let herself fall under the waves, she'd wanted them to carry her away for she was crying inside. She had done that a lot lately. Sam Andersen pressed the remote and went upstairs.

Nestled between lacy, flesh-coloured bras were several sheets of water stained papers. She carefully picked them up as if they were made of gold. It was only half past eight, another evening home alone, she thought. Shaun would be on the ferry. Lately, Keith was either on the gas rig or spending his new found wealth on fishing tackle. He wouldn't be back until dawn with his catch.

She pondered over the ripped-out diary pages. The image of Darren, as she called him, had blurred over the years. Certain features, his dark eyes, his smile, were there, but she couldn't quite remember his whole face. She wondered if he were to reappear in her life she would recognise him at all. Always too embarrassed to pronounce his real name, she didn't even know what his full name was.

Suddenly she heard a noise, and she shouted out: 'Ah!' Her heart pounded against her tight leotard. Through the nets she watched rockets dart up into the night sky. Shaun still seemed like her baby, yet it was hard to believe that she had only been a year older than him when she had fled to Amsterdam.

At first Sam had wandered around the city. Everywhere pointed to the promise of spring. It was just around the corner. Free to roam at last. No Mum shouting obscenities in the middle of the night, or wandering down to the sea in her pink nylon nightie, and most painful of all - no Dad to go and search for Mum before she, unable to swim, stepped into the water.

Sam was anonymous in Amsterdam. No-one stopped to give her a second look. She looked like everyone else, in her Lycra leggings and baggy T-shirts. Nelleke and Arnold were kind. They gave her a door key and as many Guilders as she wanted.

The early mist gone, the afternoon sun was warm as she sat down and listened to one of the many street musicians. The square was full of happy voices and music.

It reminded her of days in Norwich. Visiting Jonathan on The Street, as everyone called Dundee Street, and meeting his friends. Every day that summer Sam made her way through the city to The Street. It was a street you either loved or loathed. It was often in the news and great placards read 'squatters' rights'. Darren, like a guru, was always surrounded by admiring young girls in hippy skirts and angry punks seeking solace.

Around mid afternoon they would wander hand in hand by the river Waveney; they would stop and paddle, carefree like toddlers. They no longer asked each other about their families. Each had their own reason for forgetting them. Sam believed Darren's to be the more noble choice. For back in his home town, bombs fell and boys much younger than him were being sent to war. Money had stopped coming some time ago and he funded his own studies with early morning cleaning of city offices. She on the other hand had both her parents, although Dad was hanging on in there for dear life, unable to speak or move. Once she'd taken Darren to the hospital with her. She knew Dad wouldn't be able to disapprove in his now silent world.

In the ward, Sam quizzed her Dad desperate to find out where he stored all the paperwork for the house. He seemed unable to recognise her. At best he would grunt, usually he said nothing. Sam had gone out to take care of some things. She left Darren with him. He didn't know quite what to say. He took out a box of food he'd prepared for himself and Sam.

'I'm going to eat some pilaf, I hope you don't mind.' The old man followed his every mouthful, the fragrant rice smelling of comfort. Then he grabbed a spoonful and ate it. Darren was so surprised he carried on feeding the man.

'Good. You good,' he said. Darren never visited the hospital again, for the following week the old man was dead. And Sam stopped visiting The Street.

Soon after that The Street, its row of terraced houses, was blown to the ground. To make room for new, decent housing, that was what the news had said. She never saw Darren again. How life was different then, she pondered. Mobiles were yet to be invented, and her parents refused to have a phone at home, 'a waste of money', they'd said. For maybe, just maybe, she would have found out where he went. Things might have turned out differently.

Jonathan was her only connection to that time. After The Street was demolished he moved back home, like the scared son he always was. So scared, it turned out that he told his mother the whole story of Sam and Darren just in case his mother thought it was him who had got her pregnant.

Chapter 11

I pushed on the glass door of the hostel. It was locked. I rang on the bell. A pale girl with dyed black hair opened the door.

'You staying here? What's your name? Got some ID?'

'Shaun Andersen,' I said, feeling guilty, fiddling with my empty wallet. I pulled out my Student Union card. The girl studied my embarrassing mug shot.

'Shame about the picture!' she smirked. 'There's a message here for you, Shaun Andersen,' she said, in her deep, husky voice. I took the note from her red-taloned hands and made my way to the dormitory.

Shaun,

please notify Tassy or myself as soon as you're back, whatever the time.

Dave.

I knocked quietly on Dave's door. Loud snores bellowed out through the keyhole. I knocked harder.

'What the f**k is up,' he said opening the door. I looked down and up again, he was stark naked. I began to jiggle from one foot to the other. The room was so white and plain there was nowhere to look, except at Dave.

'Just a moment,' he said cool as a cucumber, and put on a towelling dressing gown. I'd almost forgotten why I was there, when there was some noise in the corridor and Tassy arrived. She looked different, older. It took me a while to realise what it was. She wasn't wearing any make-up.

Strange, though, as I never thought she wore make-up.

'My money's gone,' was all I said holding up my empty wallet, which was true. It had the desired effect. 'I had to walk back,' I said, unable to look either of them in the face.

'Oh my God!' exclaimed Tassy, 'he's been mugged!'

'Mmm,' said Dave, cringingly stroking his beard. 'Shouldn't have been out wandering the streets on your own. You could have phoned us. We rang you. You'd switched your phone off.'

'It's gone.' I emptied out my pockets as theatrically as I could, pulling out the fabric to reveal old tissues, bus tickets and pony tail bands.

'They took my phone as well,' I said, which again was true - well sort of.

'We'd all best get some sleep now. We'll discuss this further in the morning,' said Dave, as sternly as anyone could wrapped in a white hand towel.

I crept into the boys' dorm. It was dark and smelt stale and airless just like the changing rooms at Gt Waveney High. I crept along, thinking they were all asleep.

'Woo hoo. Look what the cat's dragged in.' said Nikki,

'Going to tell us what you've been up to? Had a good time then?' winked Miki.

I shrugged and went to bed.

A voice pounded at the door.

'Time to get up,' shouted Dave. 'Need to talk to you Shaun. On your own. Down in reception in five minutes.' I arrived first and waited under the watchful eye of the Goth girl as she re-painted her nails.

'So where were you last night?' said Dave.

'Dunno. Just got lost.'

'We almost called your parents you know. Had you on the next ferry out.' If any of what really happened got out I knew my chances with Alice would be zilch. Yet I had mixed feelings. Part of me wished last night had never happened; part of me was relieved that I had joined the ranks of Miki. Most of the other guys said they'd slept with girls; we all made it up, in a really vague way, with just enough detail taken from books and films to convince each other.

'I'm sorry. It won't happen again,' I mumbled.

'Too right it won't. You haven't got any money now, either. Is that right?' I nodded. 'Just a one-off incident,' continued Dave, winking at me. I felt my stomach lurch. I couldn't get the naked image of Dave out of my head. I don't remember ever seeing Mum and Dad naked, or even in their underwear for that matter.

'Well, I'm going have to set an example. You're grounded for the morning. You'll miss the Rijksmuseum and flea market.' I was about to argue my case with Dave. I didn't really care about the flea market. What would I be buying, with no money?

I yawned my way through breakfast. I didn't have an appetite. I felt like a walking advertisement for what had happened at the bar, I was sure that everyone somehow knew that I gave off some sort of aura of my adventure. Although of course I realised later it was a brothel, or whatever you call it, rather than a Happy Hour bar that I believed I'd entered. I watched Miki chat to Alice, in that slimy way of his, getting really close, like a pervert. If he wasn't so good looking, if it was Anthony Rix they'd all be complaining. Then Miki switched his attention to Tassy.

'You look really pretty this morning, Tassy,' he said.

'Thanks, you've made my day,' she said, looking away.

'Ready to go, mate,' said Nikki.

'I'm grounded,' I said. I watched them go out and wondered what on earth I was going to do all morning.

'Here you are,' said Dave, handing me a work sheet. 'Plenty to keep you busy!'

'Dorms are out of bounds 9.30-4pm,' said the Goth. 'You can stay in the reception, if you like,' she grinned at me, revealing a gold tooth.

I took out my sketchbook and Mum's diary from my 'man bag', as Nikki called my new leather shoulder bag. I flicked through my sketch book; it fell open at the drawing of the nameless girl. I banged it shut. Should I throw it away? Yet it was one of my best drawings ever. I took out the diary and opened it where I'd left my ruler. I'd hated these blue rulers at school. 'Thickos' rulers, coz they can't read,' taunted the bullies. Who cares, no-one knows me in Amsterdam, I thought. The hostel quietened down and I began to read.

Sam Colby's Diary

March 21st 1985
Nelleke and Arnold are really kind, maybe too kind. Arnold is quite good looking too, he's tall with an angular well defined face, a bit like David Bowie. Too old for my liking, he's nearly forty! But something's starting to give me the creeps. Something feels not quite right. I do feel sorry for them not being able to have children. I'm their last chance, before they really are too old to be parents. There are not many children to adopt here, especially babies. Maybe I'm imaging that Nelleke and Arnold are weird. But they don't even seem to argue. Mum and Dad were always at it. Well, come to think about it, Mum really. It seems very quiet here. No-one visits except Arnold's father, Mr. 'de Moye' - as everybody called him after the flower company. And another thing, almost anything starts me off crying nowadays.

April 5th 1985
I'm feeling really sleepy all the time now. The other day I wondered if Nelleke and Arnold had drugged me. Or am I going mad?

A postcard marked the page. Shaun looked at the dented Golden Mile with its fake summer blue sea and sky. It said:

Dear Samantha,

I've told everyone you've got glandular fever and you've gone to stay with a distant relative, seeing as the state your mum's in. And that you need looking after.

Yours faithfully Glynis Plumb

I turned the card round and round to read the miniscule writing around the edge of the card.

PS Sam, I hope you're ok. I think you've done the right thing. I haven't found out what happened to D, but I guess he didn't have the right papers, I think his visa ran out some time ago, and with the police demolishing the squat he made a quick exit.

JP

April 12th

As I walked past the last of the busy canals before home, as I now think of Nelleke and Arnold's house. I thought of Darren and our summer walks by the river seemed so long ago. Here, other young couples, tourists have flocked here for Easter. Darren has gone. He's disappeared off the face of the earth. Maybe Tao was right that day I saw her rattling across the bridge with all her worldly goods in a tartan shopping trolley. We both looked down on the rubble which had been The Street.

I walked with her to the station, along the river bank. Tao said it was time to move on, it had been the fate of her people forever and life was best that way, not staying put,'for everything is transient in passing,' she said it was an ancient Buddhist quote. I didn't really get what she meant. She must have guessed from my puzzled expression and said, 'it's about living in the moment, for what else is there, everything however good will come and go.' We emptied several pots of stewed tea in the station buffet. I'd always been fascinated by her in the squat. She was the only Russian I'd ever met and seemed really exotic and mysterious. Tao wasn't her real name, but as with Darren we'd gotten used to making our own names - our own world which had been shattered by the bulldozers. She took my hands in hers; I gazed into almond eyes, perched on high cheekbones. The wrinkles around her eyes and mouth needed a little touching up I thought. It was impossible to tell her age - anything from thirty to fifty. Whatever her age I was amazed that she'd preferred to spend the summer camped out in a tent in Darren's garden. Even the squats were a relative luxury to her tiny canvas tent.

'I'll tell you your fortune,' she said. I grinned, thinking of Mystic Meg on the sea front. Margaret was no mystic, 'they all come wanting to know something, usually about their love life; if they're married will they have kids? Men like to know about their job, promotion prospects. A pretty predictable lot really,' she'd chuckled in Mum's kitchen, whilst counting out her dosh.

'Sit still!' ordered Tao, in her rich dusky voice. I nervously talked about the weather, winter coming, as she shuffled the cards. Tao's gaze sent shivers through my spine as she reminisced about life on the Russian steppes, her child-hood

and youth spent wandering and camping in real winter weather that was minus thirty degrees. I shuffled the bright hand painted cards and passed them back to Tao. The Russian swiftly arranged the cards; she then scooped them up and arranged them in several more combinations.

'You're guarding a secret,' were the first words out of her thin mouth. 'This one - won't be yours to care for - he'll come later. You'll cross the sea to find his true home.'

'Go on,' I said, excited by the revelation about Darren.

The cards seemed to fly past me: musicians on rooftops, angels, flying horses. They were bordered with decorative and illegible letter forms. Tao muttered to herself in deep, foreign syllables. She then left this trance-like state and doled out her predictions:

'You'll conceive a child, a boy. He's not yours to raise. He's life's longing for itself. His parents have already been chosen. They say it's not your job, but in time a boy, a baby boy, and then you'll be happy. But seek not to make him like you..................then, what's the word, an unrequited love. There's a moving sea between the shores of your souls. The wind blows and restless are the sails. And remember my girl that yesterday is but a memory and tomorrow is today's dream. You'll know who he is from his talent, his talent for cooking.' Tearfully, I passed Tao almost all my money, except my train fare and ran to board the Gt Waveney train.

Now I'm here across the sea, I don't think she was talking about Darren, but his son. I'm sure it will be a son.

'The strange thing is,' Tao went on, 'he'll come back to you much later, when you've settled your life.'

Who's Darren? Mum's never mentioned a Darren. And typical Mum off to the psychic. I could hear Dad's voice. 'Waste of money each new craze of hers. Pilates, reflexology, astrology - load of rubbish, hey mate.' I always agreed, not sure what I was agreeing to. Yet part of me knew that it was like Mystic Meg on the pier; we all knew she made it up for the holiday makers, except for that one time, before Dad's accident at the turkey farm. How did she know that?

'Something wrong mate?' said the Goth.
I shook my head and buried myself further into the book.

Spring is everywhere. And everywhere I see Darren: reflections in the canal, I follow someone, but as they turn around I know it isn't him. It's impossible to look at my reflection and see anything other than a lonely girl with a nine month bump.

'What!' I exclaimed out loud, suddenly realising why she went to Amsterdam. My thought flitted about. How could she have not told me? I'd always wanted a brother or sister. I remembered when I was about six or seven and Mum and Dad asking me what I wanted for Christmas.

I'd said, 'I'd like a brother or sister.' Mum hadn't said anything. She just got up and left the room. Dad had just laughed it off. I remember him saying:

'She wasn't very well when she was pregnant with you. Up here. You know,' he'd said tapping his head. I'd had no idea what he'd meant then. But like one of my enormous sea puzzles, only I can do, the pieces were starting to make a picture. For the first time ever, I wanted to **read** more. I had to know what happened next.

Sam Colby's Diary

April 15th 1985

I'm having loads of weird dreams. It must be all this sleeping in the day. I pull down my blinds and shut out the springtime and lie in darkness all day. This afternoon I dreamt I was floating weightlessly through water. I was the only person in the river. Around the edge was all the old gang from The Street: Jonathan, Darren, and Tao. They stared at me. Their voices were muffled, as if lost through time. I could make out 'Samantha lost, gone.'

April 17th 1985

Nelleke and Arnold are on tenterhooks. Every time the phone rings or there's a knock on the door, they exchange glances and look at me. Last night Arnold paced up and down the floor, I heard them arguing in that throaty Dutch sound I cannot get my tongue round. I hid in my room, and began to wonder if Nelleke and Arnold are just pretending to be nice? If not why all these furtive looks, arguments and whispered phone calls, as if I could understand them anyway! She's so tall and elegant, really cool looking. I feel a fat, frump next to her in her trendy ski pants. Arnold looks just like all the other Dutchmen, tall, fair and with this strong chin, like a comic book super hero. He says exactly what he thinks to people. Dad would have thought him so rude. But that seems the way of things here.

.Then the bombshell was dropped today. Marga, the midwife came to visit. Guess what! I'm going to have the baby at home. I can't believe Mum would go along with this - if she knew. Mum loves hospitals and doctors and all that attention. She thinks the National Health Service is the eighth wonder of the world. Apparently home births have remained popular here, but who knows what is true anymore. To be honest, I just can't imagine how the baby's going to get out! Of course I know the biology, but I'm so enormous now I can't imagine the baby outside of me.

After that I sneaked out to the canal. Sneak seems the operative word. They seem to be watching my every move. By the canal there was no escape from the smell of spring. I hated the pink apple blossom, the sweet smell from the white lilac tree. I hated what this spring had in store for me. I hated my fat belly and the shoves and kicks inside of it. But even more I loathed what would happen once the baby was out.

April 18th 1985
Pieter was born at five o' clock in the morning - on Good Friday. We all agreed on the

name. He's gorgeous. A big boy 1.85 kg or nine pounds exactly, as I had it converted. It started with the most agonising period pains ever. When I thought that was as bad as things could get, then this razor like sensation as if I was being ripped apart. I'll never complain when I'm ill again! Thank God it's all over. I'm so tired I can't write anymore.

I began to feel really weird at that point. It's bad enough knowing that Mum and Dad had sex once to conceive me. But who was this Darren? And this giving birth stuff is disgusting. Yet I wanted to read on.

Sam Colby's Diary

May 12th 1985
Nelleke and Arnold are running around like mad attending to Pieter's every need. He's so fragile, I want to bundle him up and run off somewhere. But there's nowhere to go. I am a spare part now. I know they want me to go home. They keep giving me money to go out. I'm a permanent fixture at the cinema. I've seen 'Room with a View' six times now. Full of beautiful people and exotic landscapes, for whom it all works out right in the end. I keep thinking if I wish and pray enough, all will be well.

May 13th 1985

Two big shocks today. Mr. 'de Moye' is going to England on Monday night, with me in the back of the van. I asked about all the documents I thought I'd have to sign. I'd heard something about going to court in England when you adopt. That was when it all got really fishy. Arnold said that was all taken care of. I needn't worry myself. When Marga came in to weigh and check Pieter I asked her. She looked into the kitchen and waited until Nelleke was busy making up baby bottles in the kitchen.

'I'm a private mid-wife private. So I don't really know much about these things. No one knows about you or Peter,' she whispered. Nelleke came back in grinning.

'What have you two been chatting about,' she asked.

'Just admiring this lovely boy,' she said.

So there's just the four of them that know the truth: Nelleke, Arnold and Marga, and Mr. de. Moye if he counts.

I couldn't bear to stay in the house any longer, watching, looking at Pieter. I know that sounds awful. I found myself downtown and wandering into a tattooists. 'World Class Tattoos,' I thought of Dad and Granddad. They'd go down to Joe Vasselli's on Britannia pier and come back with hearts and anchors on their arms. It was strictly men only. I'd never have dreamt of going in.

I took a seat, wanting it to hurt, to be punished with the needle. I wanted a bleeding heart. The little man in the shop kept shaking his head and said I'd regret it. 'I've had too many love sick girls and boys here. They come back a week later wanting someone else's initials. I'll do a bleeding heart which will always look beautiful and remind you of Amsterdam.' I didn't have the will or energy to disagree. After the heat and a sudden tightness across the top of my buttock I saw the reflection of a tulip.

That's where the diary stopped. There was a letter on faint lined paper wedges into the last page.

Dear Shaun,

Well done if you get this far. I know you'll think I'm a coward not telling you any of this. I've tried so many times, but the words just never came out. Then when you said about the trip I wanted you to know. Things were so different then, back in the 80s. It wasn't the liberated world you live in today, certainly not in Gt Waveney. Nan was in hospital and well, there wasn't anyone else I could turn to. Mrs. Plumb, sort of took over. Jonathan and I were at school together and he was my best mate. It was through him I met Piieter's father. There's another reason I've given you this. I want you to find Pieter. I promised all those years ago that I wouldn't. And I'll keep to it. I guess I'm too superstitious not to. But you Shaun. You and Peter have a right to know each other. This is the address where they lived and the name of the flower van. They may have all moved on. Whatever you do, do this alone. We don't want Dad knowing. Not yet.
Lots of love
Mum

PS About the tattoo, I know I banned you from having one and you'll think I'm a hypocrite - it's just there's no going back. It's branded on you forever.

'Are you all right? You look a bit pale,' said the Goth girl.

'Sure. I'm fine,' I said, my hands trembling as I put down the book.

I rushed into the gents and looked at my face in the smudged mirror. Was there someone out there who looked like me? Did he have my grey eyes or my mousy blond hair? I rolled up my sweatshirt and I looked at the map on my arm, as I called my scar; my own mark or branding of the Colby tribe. The doctor called it vitiligo. I was about four when I first noticed it. The pale river-like lines which never tan. I remember it clearly for it was the same day Mum lost it.

It was a rare hot day. The sun never gets as far as Gt Waveney. Mum took me to the park, which was unusual in itself. Dad, the only child's playmate, usually took me everywhere. Which meant I spent most of my childhood on the beach.

That day I'd taken my new boy doll to the park. It looked like a real baby. I didn't normally play with dolls, and never again after Mum's episode. Nan had won this doll on the bingo. It had real eyelashes and rolling eyes. Being the only grandchild, the fact I was a little boy didn't matter - it had to be mine.

I carried him up the ladder and gently nudged him. A woman screamed,

'Look there's a baby coming down the slide,'

'It's Peter. My baby Peter,' I shouted back, before whizzing down the burning metal after him. Mum grabbed me off the slide; she shook me and shouted,

'You stupid, stupid boy!' She tossed the doll into a bin. I cried all the way home. No Peter doll and no ice cream.

I splashed some cold water over my face, realising that life would never be the same again.

Chapter 12

When the group came back at dusk the hostel immediately sprang to life. The only people I really noticed were Alice and Miklos. They chatted away as if they'd known each other forever.

'Stop moping around!' laughed Miklos, pointing at me. I'd never truly felt jealousy until that moment. You see movies about guys getting into fights over girls and at that moment I could have gone for him.

I'm not sure what stopped me, probably my memory of sleeping over at the twins' house. His bedroom wall was a shrine to himself. Photos of Miklos, like bizarre wallpaper, covered every inch of the wall. I knew who he loved most. Alice didn't stand a chance! So, instead of punching him, I banged about noisily making my way up to the dorm.

It was quiet inside. Everyone had gone out, or so I thought. A shudder went through me, I wasn't alone. I watched Rixy as he carefully folded all our clothes, even my Primark T-fronts were carefully placed on my bunk. He then started on the art equipment, picking up pencils and sorting rolls of paper. I watched him sort all the coloured pencils into a perfect rainbow. I jumped, hearing a tap on the door.

'Can I come in?' whispered Alice, peeping round the door. I jumped up like an obedient dog. She came over and we sat down, both mesmerized by Rixy's folding and stacking.

'I thought you'd gone with the others - for the Indonesian meal?'

'I had a change of plan,' she said looking me right in the eye. Why? I thought, yet before I knew it I'd said out loud,

'Why?'

'It's just all been such good fun starting at Art School, it's made me feel a bit down. Do you know what I mean?' she asked. I shook my head. At first I didn't have a clue what she meant. Then, snapshots of summer in Gt Waveney clicked into my head. I saw the lumps of tanned flesh parading up and down the Golden Mile.

'You know I hate the summer, when everybody is happy. It makes me hot, irritable and I don't even tan,' I said rolling up my sleeve and showing her my vitiligo.

'It looks like a map,' she said tracing the pale lines with her fingertips.

'Exactly. That's what I called it when I was a kid.'

Rixy screeched and dragged art boxes across the room and stacked them up like a supermarket of art equipment. The spell was broken,

'Are you hungry?' asked Alice. 'I know of a very good restaurant.'

I sipped my beer and focused on Alice as she ordered for the two of us.

'I was brought up in a poky flat above Dad's restaurant 'The Shah of Persia', a bit like this place' she said. This threw me. I imagined her living in some posh house, big sunny windows and velvet fabrics like the TV cook, Nigella. I could see Alice in a red satin dressing gown tasting something delicious and licking her full red lips, just like Nigella. She didn't belong in a little flat above a restaurant.

'But I thought you'd been to some posh girls' school,' I said.

'Oh, that. I wanted to go to an ordinary school with ordinary people where I could relax and have fun. But Dad had other ideas. He thought it would be good for me to go to a fancy all girls' school. The school put me under so much pressure. They used to say to me, 'We've only had one B in the last five years, don't be the second.' We'd predict who was going to get what score before a test. Even when I did do well I was never satisfied and dwelt on what I'd got wrong.'

'Didn't you enjoy it? I always thought clever people just liked doing that kind of stuff. If not, why bother.'

'Shaun, it's not that simple. Winning is all that mattered.'

'Yeah, but when I am doing art or designing the cakes I'm nor trying to win anything. I just like doing it.'

'Well you're luckier than all these rich kids. We were just on a hamster treadmill. You can see now that by the time I reached the sixth form all I could think about was getting out.'

'You make it sound like a prison!' I joked.

'It was,' she answered. 'I was one of two girls doing art A level. Of course I had to do three other subjects as well! Art wasn't seen as a proper subject. Dad wouldn't hear of me going to Art School. The only way out was to apply for university - and do art history. '

Tiny wedges of herb omelette arrived. She carried on talking. I carried on eating. 'I was the only one in the whole school who lived in a place like the 'Shah of Persia'. Dad wasn't really a cook, but a chemist, you know, a pharmacist.' I thought of the Indian man in Boots the chemist; they always seemed to be foreigners like Alice's dad.

'We were well off then, but something happened,' she looked down at the table.

'Did **you** like **your** school?' she asked, changing the subject completely.

'No way!' I said, which was truly an understatement. Yet I did have some good mates, it was just the reading and writing. You thought you were dumb if you got a B. Well, try being in the bottom set for everything! 'I just went to an ordinary school - Gt Waveney bog standard High School.'

'That's why I chose Gt Waveney Art School - because it is ordinary. It's real. Why are you laughing?'

'It's just I can't imagine anyone wanting to go to Gt Waveney,' I explained.

'You see when I went up to Cambridge it was like school - only worse. Most people in my school were rich. Magdalene College was for the super rich. Is your family rich?' she asked.

'You really are joking now!' I said, almost choking on my omelette. She'd seen Nan's bed & breakfast, which certainly was even more basic than our youth hostel. 'No we're absolutely working class. Mum's a secretary. And Dad - well he'd been out of work for a while,' I said thinking of the rust heap he has for a car. 'There's usually a bit of a role reversal in our house. Mum dresses up in her black pencil skirt and high heels. A bit weird really, as her boss wears jeans. Dad's always been a bit of a house husband,' I laughed. 'But now he's got a job it'll be all change.'

I thought of Miklos, the Mavroudis's were the only rich people that I knew, living up there in their big old house on the cliff top. Was she looking for that? I wondered. 'We live in a terraced house,' I said. 'And if I want to stay at college I've got to work as well.'

'Ah, the bakery,' she said.

'How do you know I work at the Upper Crust?' She just grinned back at me. Lots of different little plates of food came and went.

'Well, at Cambridge,' Alice went on, 'at first it was amazing. My room was more of an apartment. It was like being back at school, except some of the people were super rich and I was with them 24/7,' she said. 'Like, if someone suggested that we do something, I didn't want to say, I can't afford it,' she continued. 'They were very nice, good girls who should all have been at a vicar's tea party. They were much shallower than I expected. All their conversations were about shoes or having the right bag to go to the right club.'

'Perhaps that's all they've got to talk about,' I suggested.

'They weren't interested in their courses. You know, Rixy making maps of everywhere we go, just coz he wants to. It would never have occurred to them. There was just no passion there.'

I started to feel a bit embarrassed by all this talk. I knew what she meant. I was just surprised that she said it.

'But then other things started to happen in my head. So I quit Cambridge. Gt Waveney is such a relief! It's full of ordinary people.' She smiled a beautiful big lipped smile, and I thought of Nigella again. The meatballs arrived. I should have said that I was a veggie, yet I just wanted to do everything Alice's way.

'Was it just the lack of money, at Cambridge? I know what that's like,' I said, trying not to gag on the livery taste of the meatballs. 'When Dave says, 'Where's your sketchbook?' he doesn't realise I don't have a grant or a loan to buy a sleek black book like Miklos. Mine's from the pound shop.' I felt I was rambling and Alice kept looking distractedly around at the other diners.

'So what did happen? How did you end up at Art School?' I asked.

'What you really want to know is why I left Cambridge. What those funny things in my head were?'

'I'll listen to you anytime,' I said, really meaning it.

'I'm not sure when I first met Will.' Oh no, I thought, it's going to be a boyfriend story - about someone way out of my league.

'It was probably when he was busking just before Christmas,' she went on. 'He was good. Really good. One thing I had loved at St Mary's was the singing. He sang and played the violin. He wasn't your stereotype handsome, in his tatty clothes. He was just like no one else I knew in Cambridge, or anywhere else. I just stood there, at first not sure if it was him or the music that cast me into the spell.'

'Sounds more like the Pied Piper,' I said. Alice blanked me and carried on,

'I don't know how long I'd stood there, it began to drizzle, and he finally put his violin away and closed up shop. "Fancy coming for a drink? You can help me count my hoard," he said. There was something forbidden and pirate-like about Will. I guess we looked an odd pair, when we walked into Aunty's Teashop. I looked a typical Cambridge student: jeans, blazer and Magdalene college scarf.'

'Sounds like a uniform,' I said. 'Did you know Nikki calls you a 'hippy chick? All your patterned and sparkly fabrics.' Alice grinned.

'And of course Will was grunge unlimited. It was hard to tell how long ago it was when he'd last got a comb through his matted, blond hair.

'That's men for you,' I laughed, desperately not trying to sound jealous. Plates of miniature sticky cakes arrived. 'Go on,' I said.

'You see he, Will, was old. Forty-two actually. Old enough to be my father,' she said in a mocking sing-song voice. 'After the tea and scones he invited me back to his place.' At this point I wasn't sure that I wanted Alice to carry on. The whole story started to seem so unlikely. *Was she telling the truth?* I wondered. My mind felt scrambled. I couldn't keep up with the order of Alice's events.

'This is my home,' Will announced, undoing the padlock to a removal van. It was like the Tardis, much bigger inside.

'And you were Dr Who's assistant?' I said, trying to lighten her mood. Something told me that this story was leading to something awful. And there was no way out for me, other than running out of the restaurant, which in truth I wasn't brave enough to do.

'Inside were crimson oriental rugs and fabrics from India which still carried their sweet, exotic perfume. Propped against Stop the War posters were stringed musical instruments, most of which I'd never seen before. The van was bathed in a sweet, damp wooden smell. The smell I so loved about him was all around me then.' I tried to conceal a laugh which spluttered into a hiccupy cough. Maybe I was embarrassed by all that gooey and romantic stuff.

'Inside it had none of the mod cons of camping life.'

'I used to clean caravans at Birchwood holiday park, did it all summer,' I said. She smiled at me as if I was twelve or something.

'Will's van was full of tools, machines, bits of wood and so on. I'd never seen anything like it. At my school it was a miracle if anyone did art. CDT was banned. The boys I'd met at Cambridge couldn't put up a shelf, let alone make something as perfectly and beautiful as Will did.'

I bit into the honey cake, Alice talked. *What are the ingredients? What are they called?* I wondered. She just talked and talked and there seemed no point in stopping or asking her anything about the food.

'I spent more and more time with Will. I became his apprentice, in lots of ways.' I smirked, quickly brushing my hands across my face, whilst images of the girl from the Happy Hour bar shot through my head. I thought of Lauren; why had I snogged her at a school disco? Alice was different. Would there ever be an Alice and me? I listened as my chances grew slimmer by the minute.

'There are more Big Issue sellers in Cambridge than anywhere else in the country! Did you know that?' Before I could answer, she went on, 'Will wasn't exactly homeless, but knew a lot of the people on the streets. They blanked me when I was with Will, I became the invisible girl they never spoke to.

'During the Lent term - that's what they call spring term at Cambridge, I saw more and more of Will. I turned down numerous invites to shooting parties and country house weekends to busk with him on a Saturday afternoon. I didn't fit in with the Cambridge lot anyway. Yet, to be honest I didn't really fit in with Will. Sometimes I saw him at a distance with other girls. Yet what could I say? He'd made it clear I'd never be the only one. I was number one, but not the only one.

'I got more and more behind with my work. When the May ball came I invited Will, initially on impulse, but later, when I had time to think about it all, I guess I thought I would impress everyone. Will would be my novelty, my party piece. And for one night only he'd be all mine.

'As the ball got closer I started to get more and more anxious. I was behind with my revision and had this sense of foreboding. Like when you hear scary music in a film, you know something awful is going to happen next. Through the long light nights of May I slept very little. When I did sleep I'd wake hearing a loud orchestra playing. I'd run to the television, the CD player - yet they were all switched off.

'I needn't have worried about Will, he scrubbed up pretty good. But all evening I expected him to put a foot wrong. He didn't. He was like a male Cinderella; clean shaven, hired suit,' she laughed. 'We walked in and heads really did turn. I had butterflies in my stomach. I was all set for the best night of my life.

'All was quiet for the speeches. The vice chancellor proposed a toast to the college and the endowment from Jetty's, an old city firm. Up onto the podium strode Graham. He scanned the audience with his lop-sided smile. Before I knew it my champagne flute was in smithereens on the grass.

'That night I went to bed and couldn't get up again. My dreams got louder. I'd wake in the night hearing drums, violins, and a full orchestra. The night of the ball I threw the telly through the window. Marian, the house matron was called. The year before her son had thought he was John the Baptist. Rumour had it he heard voices and could be seen catching and eating bugs in the botanic garden. So I was only a minor challenge. She tucked me into bed, like a little child. Mum came for me. I went home and never saw Will again. He didn't believe in mobiles. Too many dangerous masts. He was a bit of a technophobe. There's no way I can find him. He went off somewhere with some other travellers - their latest campaign. Shaun, you look puzzled?'

'I'm sorry, Alice. What happened to you and all that,' I said. What I was really thinking was that my terrors were all out in the world. The dunce. The thicko. Remedial. Special Needs. Yet for Alice and her kind, it was all invisible.

'If you'd like to hear the rest I'll tell you tomorrow night. It's a long story - and I realise now that I've left the beginning out. It's too long for one sitting. So what about you, Shaun? Tell me all.' I wanted to tell Alice about Mum's diary and letter, but I just went numb. Maybe secrets are like that. Once you've told one person you can tell someone else. So I lied. I just said the usual stuff about my God damn dull and ordinary family. How I was the first person to go to college. She seemed to really find it interesting, and kept saying she'd never met anyone like me before. And of course I was flattered.

Chapter 13

I spent the whole day just thinking about seeing Alice. I was sure everybody knew I was obsessed with her. The morning dragged on forever. I wandered the large galleries of Stadelijk Museum, unable to really look at any of the giant canvases. I gazed at the great black outlines of abstracted faces and bodies. They were coloured in with bright, blobby paint. In them I saw Alice with this Will guy, the happy hour girl and faces from the red light district and maybe someone like me.

'A penny for your thoughts,' said Tassy.

'You can see all kinds of people, things. Can't you?' I asked, anxious that she might laugh at me.

'It's phenomenology.'

'What?' I answered.

'You must have looked up at a cloud and saw a dragon racing across the sky,'

'Or a skull, a face,' I answered.

'Exactly,' she said. 'We see what's racing through our own mind,' wandering into the next gallery. At least she didn't ask me if I needed a note-taker. My mind often ran ahead of me, and there was never the time to write it all down. Tassy was right today, this phenomena thing. Everything I saw reminded me of Alice in one way or another. Then I'd see someone who looked a little like me and I thought of this half brother of mine.

'Shaun, can you keep a secret?' I looked around the café, not really expecting to see anyone I knew, and nodded.

'Of course I can. Cross my heart and hope to die,' I gesticulated. It made her laugh. Each time Alice laughed I felt responsible for it, and I felt good.

The waiter slammed down two cups of coffee. I'd really wanted a Coca Cola, with a great long stripy straw, but I thought it made me sound like a big kid. Alice always wanted to be in a bar or café. Until then, I never went to places like that. I might buy a veggie burger and eat it wandering back home along the sea front. Our family didn't do cafés - well that's not completely true. Dad's idea of a treat, like when Mum passed her driving test, was to drive us to the Little Chef for a fry up - Dad's definitely the last of the big spenders. Of course I couldn't tell Alice. And I could see the hostel across the road, which meant the others could see me. *Shaun the cool!* I thought.

'What I told you about Will. It's true that knowing him and what happened forced my hand in leaving Cambridge. It's just that it never started there. It all started in the sixth form.' Nobody ever spoke to me like this before. I felt as if I was in some television chat show, where the guests reveal all. At home Mum and Dad were nice enough parents. But they never talked to me the way Alice did. If Dad was cross he'd say the F-word. The nearest Mum came to showing her feelings would be smashing a plate on the cooker. Nan, though, was another case entirely. There were jokes, rumours, really, about the time she threw the television at Granddad or worse still, the day she tried to run him over in her old Escort. Granddad brushed it off saying, 'she's a crap driver.'

'I've got a confession to make too,' I said. 'You go first.'

'No, you,' said Alice. We went on like that for some time. Eventually Alice, began.

'We often went to Perkins & Jones after school. That is, me, Saskia and Dotty. We'd try and get the window seats and look down on Oxford Street. It seemed alive with all the shoppers and tourists. I believed life was elsewhere. Certainly not in the classroom. We were in the sixth form. Finally free of our tartan kilts, shirts and ties. We felt superior in just the school colours: olive green, beige and brown. I never, ever wear those colours now.'

'I was never one for my uniform. I used to customise it with drawings of skulls and daggers,' I added. Alice smiled and touched my hand. She just seemed so perfect. I thought back to the episode with the prostitute. *Should I tell her about it?* If I was on a TV show that would be the sort of thing I'd say.

'I'll be honest with you,' she said. 'I think it all began when it was my turn to pay.'

I suddenly thought back to a few days ago at the Sunrise Café, Alice buying the donuts, it seemed far more than a couple of days ago.

'Dotty and Saskia had bagged the best seats by the window, overlooking the shoppers – you never knew who you might spot,' she continued. 'It was that horrible, empty time: all Christmas lights were gone. It was dark on the way to school and after school, and we were in the midst of our mock A levels. It was pretty bleak. I emptied out my purse, unable to cough up the cash for the lattes and little squares of chocolate. We always liked to comfort ourselves with chocolate,' she said looking down at our plates of gooey chocolate cake. 'Awfully bad luck. Happened to me once at Fortnum's,' said an old man at the opposite till. 'Add it on to my bill, would you be so kind,' he instructed the cashier. I smiled and said thank you. He bowed theatrically, his red dotted cravat and pin-stripe suit bobbed up and down. I watched him carry his pot of tea, the tray wobbling, over to the smokers section. Saskia and Dotty left early and I thought I'd do a bit of revising. I opened my book.'

'I often come here for afternoon tea. I always, see you girls on a Friday.'

'I nodded and kept my head in the book. He sat down, uninvited. I said something like,

'Don't mind if you do.' Alice laughed. I laughed too.

'I found myself telling him about Dad dying and Mum scraping together school fees to get me through my A levels. As if it hadn't been hard enough before he died. He listened, just listened. No questions. No moralising. I thought of him as a bit like the Granddad I've never had. I started going to Perkins and Jones alone, on other afternoons and Harry, that was his name, was always there. Then, one sunny spring afternoon there seemed a lightness in the air. Harry explained how he'd been thinking about my situation, having fallen on hard times. He made me sound like a Dickens character. He had a friend who needed someone to go to functions with him. It would be strictly business. They would provide a clothes allowance for me to look the part.'

'You'll be a bit like an actress,' he explained. 'It'll will solve all your money problems, get you out of the house away from all those sisters of yours,' he said.

'It was OK at first. More than OK. I strolled in to corporate events at the Tate Gallery and the Royal Academy. I've seen the art world. You see, they invite all these jerks, not that Graham was a jerk,' she said, her eyes gaining a far away look,

'Who was Graham?' I muttered under my breath, starting to lose track of all these men. Other men.

'These people aren't like us. They have no imagination. They don't even like art. They listen to the lecture about the paintings and then rush off to gorge on little canapés and endless champagne and make these great business deals.'

I nodded, not knowing why. I'd only been to London once and that was with the school. And now the mention of this old chap Harry, and whoever Graham was I started to feel like Alice's kid brother, not a potential boyfriend. Then her eyes welled up and she burst into tears. I normally hate it when girls do that, but it gave me the opportunity to grab her hand. She clasped it tight. Moving closer, I could smell her sweet, almost edible perfume.

'So when I got into Cambridge whenever I needed a bit of money, I went back to London.

Sometimes for the whole weekend, sometimes on a weekday evening, I'd take the train down to London and meet Graham, or one of Harry's friends for some special event. It was my secret. I never let on to Saskia or Dotty. They were far away anyway by that point. Saskia was having a gap year as a chalet maid in Switzerland and Dotty, always the really clever one, she had her head down at Oxford studying mathematics.'

'Do you keep secrets? It's just with secrets, once you let it out, tell one person there's no knowing where it will end.' I nodded, thinking of Mum's diary and letter.

'So I told Will. I thought with his "eye for the ladies", (not my words, Saskia's actually), that he'd be relieved that I wouldn't be following him around like a lost puppy. But he went mad. He started picking up all these tools in his workshop, I didn't know if he was going to kill me or planning to do the same to Harry. He called me all these awful names. You see, until then I'd never realised, or thought of myself as a prostitute.' Her voice faded into the background, she went on, 'but I never walked the streets and we only went to the best hotels.'

I stood up and I don't know what came over me. 'Don't you think other people have their problems? I've just found out....' My voice trailed off. I couldn't say what I wanted. Instead, I remembered some quote from school, yet when I said it came out all wrong,

'You know the vice of everything and the real you of nothing,' I garbled.

'Shaun, you've got it wrong. It's, *you know the price of everything, but the value of nothing,*' she said in her perfect, posh voice. I tipped the heavy wooden table up and like a bad magician's trick the plates and food clattered off, all over Alice.

'Shaun. What have I said? I thought you were my mate,' shouted Alice as I ran out into the street. I gazed into the canal. I kicked the railings. My head was spinning as if I'd been thrown in a tumble dryer. I wanted the railings to be Alice. She was so near to what I longed for, yet after what she said. You know it sounds silly. I guess you're thinking 'oh, she's one to have a good time with, an easy f**k'. At that point it never crossed my mind. All I could think was that I wasn't good enough for her. She'd find me dull and poor. Lauren once said, ' You're OK, quite nice, not bad looking. But you'll never have the pick of the girls.' Somewhere deep down I still believed that.

'Shaun! Shaun!' I could hear her voice, and then her distorted face and long hair swayed in the canal. I turned round. She grabbed me. I fought back then like a captured wild animal. I don't remember how long we went on like that. Eventually I ran out of steam. We found ourselves huddled together in some shop doorway. Alice was wet and sticky. She smelt of coffee and chocolate cake. I began to lick the cake off her neck.

'Tell me your secret,' she whispered. Sometimes I wish I'd asked her to carry on and tell me the rest then and there. But I didn't. She was insistent.

I told her about Mum's diary, the half brother I'd been asked to find. Alice seemed really excited, animated, her arms waving about, full of ideas of how to find him. She laid out maps and guidebooks and Mum's diary on the step.

Chapter 14

Through the sparkling windows people were chatting, a man was playing guitar. He put it away and took out a banjo. They were all laughing now. The sun hadn't quite set. Always my favourite time for nosing in on other people's houses.

'Are you sure this is the right address?' I said, baffled by the strange spellings.

'Lindeswaarstraat, the big house opposite an antique shop,' said Alice.

'Well, it isn't an antique shop anymore,' I said looking at the abstract canvases hanging in the window of the little art gallery. 'Wouldn't mind exhibiting there myself,' said Alice, adding, 'that's if I don't make it to a London gallery.

'Look!' she said, already on the steps. 'These flats all have names by the buzzers. 'Theo Meyer, Hein Gericke'. I think they must have moved on, or it's the wrong house.'

'Let's just try anyway,' I said, pressing the buzzer before the words had left my lips. Theo's buzzer. No answer. Hein's buzzer. A tall man, still holding a banjo stood at the door.

'Hello! Do you speak English?'

'Yes, a little,' he said.

'We're looking for a Peter Alferink,' I ventured. We think he may have lived here.

'I'm very sorry, no one of that name lives here.'

'Or a Peter de Moye?' asked Alice.

'I'm very sorry, no one of that name lives here either.'

Despondently we walked down the steps. To be honest I hadn't really expected to find Peter. At that moment I was more disappointed at not being one of the people at Hein's party. Life seemed elsewhere.

'Well, what now? That was our best bet,' I said .

'We could ring all the Alferinks,' suggested Alice. 'They must have phone books here, like at home.'

'And the de Moyes,' I added.

'That was a bit of a long shot. From your Mum's letters I think de Moye was only the company - not a real name.

We walked back to the hostel. We were comfortable in our silence. The group was still out. I decided to enlist the help of the Goth girl. She seemed really friendly, smiling up at me. Alice looked glum in comparison. In fact I think she was jealous, and it made me feel great. You'll be thinking I'm a real bastard, but it gave me such a buzz.

She pulled out a tatty phone book from underneath the desk. I knew that I had to find some elaborate way to get Alice to find the phone number. I still struggled to use a dictionary, so a fat phone book in Dutch was a no starter. The names wouldn't have just jumped around, they'd have done somersaults.

'I'll let you have the pleasure,' I said, thinking that I sounded like some James Bond character.

'The pleasure of what, Shaun?' she said.

'I'm not up to looking through there.'

'Oh I get it. I know it must be an emotional roller coaster, going through all this.' I nodded. I paced about like an expectant father in the old movies. Even Alice's super analytical skills couldn't find any flower company by the name of de Moye. And as for Alferink, the only Alferink listed lived out in this town called Leiden and belonged to a Hans Alferink. It was as if the family had vanished off the face of, well not the Earth, but of Amsterdam.

'Come on,' said Alice. I'll take you for a treat. In case you never get to Amsterdam again.'
'Wow! The coloured glass is amazing.'
'Genuine 1930s Art Deco,' explained Alice. The waiters glided around like swans. I felt really out of my depth. I'd never been anywhere that posh in my life.
'Are you sure you can afford this?' I said 'You know I lost all my money and everything.'
'Sure,' shrugged Alice. 'Why don't we open the letter? You never know, there might be a clue,' she said.
'But it's private - for Pieter.'
'I know but he'll never get it at this rate. Will he?' said Alice snatching it. 'I'll do the dirty deed.'
'Well you might as well read it to me then,' I snapped.

Dear Pieter,
I'm not sure where to begin. Having you adopted was the most difficult decision I have ever had to make. I was 18 when I found out I was pregnant with you. At the time my dad had just

died after a long illness and my mum was unwell in hospital. So when I met your father it was a very happy time for me. I want to tell you a little about myself. My name is Samantha and I grew up in Gt Waveney. I still live there now. They say on a clear day you can see right across to Holland. I can't tell you how many times I looked out to sea thinking of you. You must believe me that you were loved and I did what I thought best. Your father, who I called Darren was from Iran and had to leave before I could tell him about you. Darren wasn't his real name. It's not as bad as it sounds it's just that it was something like Darius. He was a kind man, studying science and a very good cook.

'Oh my God,' said Alice, beginning to tremble.

'Go on,' I said.

'Darius was my father's name - and he loved to cook.'

Before I knew it Alice slammed the letter down and ran out of the restaurant. I had no money. We seemed to be in the habit of running out on restaurants, without paying. I made a dash for it after her, but she was gone into the cold night. I clutched the letter and ran a few blocks before huddling under a street lamp and tried to read the rest.

This name business is a strange thing. Did you become Peter Alferink like your dad? Or Pieter Kostler after your mum? I remember them asking me which sounded best. 'As long as he's happy' I said. Of course back then I was Sam

Colby and now I am Sam Andersen. I got married a couple of years later and have a son named Shaun, your half brother.

I didn't read any further. I was sort of crying. I was so damn mixed up and felt kind of sick. We hadn't looked for a Pieter Kostler. I stood amidst all these happy people on the Leidseplein; drinking, chatting, and saw two distinct paths: Did I go look for Alice? Or should I try and find this Peter Kostler alone? I wished I was in a computer game and could try out both options, one after another. Nothing ever happened to me and now it was like being invited to two great parties. There was another alternative: to do nothing. I sat and watched the fire-eater, he breathed fire like some great dragon. I reached for my mobile to text Alice, but of course it was gone. I didn't even have any money for the tram, I'd relied on Alice for that. And of course there was the unpaid bill. I'd never be able to enter the American Café again.

I found myself walking back to the hostel. Inside sat the pale Goth girl. Maybe she really didn't ever sleep and was a vampire after all, for she was always there. She was always working.

'Hello again!' she announced. Her voice certainly sounded like she was from Transylvania or wherever. 'Let's see what's happened this time? Been mugged? Run over by a tram?'

'Well, if I told you the truth you simply wouldn't believe it,' I said.

'Try me. I've been around a bit. Met all sorts in this line of business.'

'You're not Dutch. Are you?' was all I could say. 'Your voice, it's ...'

'Me and all the rest of the staff aren't Dutch. I'm from Serbia. Call me Jasmina. And before you ask, your lot are all tucked up safely in their beds,' she chuckled. I felt as if time had run away with me.

'Did a girl with dark hair, Alice. Alice Nazemi come in?' She shrugged, and began filing her nails.

'Oh that girl you were here with earlier, looking up things in the phone book.'

'Yes! Yes!' I said, 'that's her.'

'Oh, I haven't seen her.' she said, completely disinterested.

'You want the truth,' I said. 'I've lost a girl who I thought was going to be my girl friend, all because she thinks my half brother is also her half brother, and we don't know where in Amsterdam he is anyway. Will that do?' I gasped.

She locked the front door.

'I'm good at finding people. I've had lots of practice,' she winked at me. This seemed a strange thing for someone a bit older than me to have been searching for people, as though that was what she did every day.

'Are you some kind of secret detective?' I found myself saying out loud. She laughed. 'How quick the world forgets one war and moves on to the next. People are creatures of habit. Let's find this brother first. She may be looking for him too. She certainly won't be looking for you.' *Why is it that foreigners are so blunt?*

'This brother - what's his name?' She asked.

'Piet.'

'Yes, but Piet what?'

'Well, that was the problem,' I began.

'Is nothing straight forward with you, mate?' she asked. I thought, yes it was until I came to Amsterdam and now life's turned into a great puzzle, which I'm not sure I'll ever be able to complete.

'I thought it was Alferink, then I thought it was de Moye, but now it's probably Kostler. Piet Kostler.'

'No. can't be. It can't be Piet Kostler.' She began to laugh. 'Piet Kostler, the performance artist. Everyone's heard of him. He was on telly a few months ago. You know that programme where they all live in one big house and are watched day and night on telly.'

'Big Brother!' I exclaimed.

'He looks nothing like you,' she said, laughing again.

'Piet Kostler. He's famous here?'

'Then it wouldn't be anything to do with my brother,' the word felt awkward, so used as I was to being an only child. 'How old is he?'

'Oh I don't know. Early twenties something like that. He calls himself a performance artist. But I'd say he's more of a magician. He stayed in the house almost to the end. Didn't win the big prize, so he's not super-rich. People just wanted to see more and more of his tricks.'

'What does he look like?'

'Show you if you like. I can't guarantee which version I'll find.' she said, typing into her computer. She turned the screen to face me. It's a woman!' I screamed, sounding a bit like a girl myself.

'It's his costume, his persona,' she said touching the sequins which lined his lips and eyes. 'Look, here's his real face.'

Instead of seeing myself, which I'd kinda vaguely hoped for, was a face so familiar, so spooky.

'Alice.' I said. The almond eyes, the mouth, almost smiling, yet a little sad, a little secretive just like the wonky Mona Lisa's smile, I thought. It's a male version of Alice. 'Are there any contact details?' I asked. 'There's a website and an e-mail address,' she said, busily typing. 'There you go, an e-mail from you to Pieter.'

'What did you say?'

'Just that you needed to see him urgently - family matters. Nice and vague,' she said.

I loitered by Jasmina, glaring at the PC. I couldn't take my eyes off the screen, I was like a trapped moth circling a light bulb, I watched each new e-mail pop onto the screen.

'There it is,' said Jasmina. 'Your answer.' She clicked on the mouse.

'It all looks double Dutch to me,' I joked, trying to disguise the feel of my heart pumping. I looked down at the words; they resembled a code or a riddle.

'So, you'd like me to translate this?' she said grinning up at me. I nodded, now feeling my pulse banging through my whole body.

'Here we go then. *Dear e-mailer, you are probably e-mailing me because you've seen me on big brother. You think you know everything about me because of the TV programme. Let me warn you now, if you believe that you are doomed.* What a cool guy,' said Jasmina.

'Yeah,' I agreed, thinking he sounded really weird. After all *Big Brother* is only a TV show. A bit of a laugh. Well that was what I thought back then.

'Then he says something about an Andy Warhol. You know this Warhol guy?' she asked, glancing up at me.

'You don't know him? Bright screen prints of Marilyn Monroe and Heinz baked bean cans. Pop Art, all sixties stuff.' I couldn't believe it - even Dad had heard of Andy Warhol, looking cool with his dark glasses and bleached hair.

She shrugged her shoulders. 'Well he didn't make it to Serbia. He goes on to say, *Andy Warhol was right, we're all being famous for fifteen minutes. Famous for everything and nothing.*'

'Go on,' I insisted, 'what else does he say?'

'He says... oh God, listen to this, anyone who wants to get in touch with him must send a hand-written letter. That's it.'

'So there's an address then?' I asked.

'Yes. But I think you should follow his instructions. Don't you?'

'What? Write a letter?' I couldn't remember the last time I'd written a letter. For one thing no one, and often that includes me, can read my hand writing and secondly I know what I want to say, but it comes out all wrong on paper. I'm still haunted by an English lesson. We were told to write a story, in joined up writing. I'd had such fun writing about this and that. I felt a real sense of achievement. The bell rang out and Mrs. Leech came over and shouted,

'Are you a complete idiot? How can anyone read this! You've joined up all the words and all the sentences. It's gibberish.'

I thought of Alice and all her fancy education. She'd be able to write an impressive letter. *Where was she?* But me? I'll probably screw up the messy paper and throw the letter in the bin.

'Well then?' said Jasmina, 'off you go.' She handed me a Hans Brenker notepad and pen. It was then that I had my idea, a brain wave. You'll think I'm bragging now, but I do have brain waves. It's like a light bulb switching on all by itself.

'I've got a better idea,' I said, now feeling that my head was above water and I was no longer drowning in the thoughts of writing a letter. 'I'll say it and you write it in Dutch,' I said handing her the notepad back. Jasmina shrugged her skinny shoulders.

'A deal. But I warn you my written Dutch isn't very good.'

'Good enough to work here,' I said trying to encourage her.

'No, Dutch people don't want to work here,' she laughed. She used that *oh aren't you a silly boy* laugh Alice had been in the habit of doing. People laughed like this usually when I thought I'd just joined the adult world.

'Dear Pieter, I don't know where to begin, other than to tell you that I am your half-brother, Shaun. I'm here in Amsterdam and need to see you. Please ring or come to the hostel.
Yours sincerely, Shaun Andersen.'

'Is that it?' she asked.

'Do you think I should say, yours faithfully, or see you soon?' I asked.

'Too late. It's done,' said Jasmina, handing me the letter, whilst carefully writing out the envelope. It was clear the letter writing was over. 'Look I'll give you a stamp, don't tell anyone.'

'I don't want a stamp,' I snapped. She rolled her charcoal eyes back at me. 'I'm going to take it myself. I haven't got time to post it.'

'You. Little boy lost. You'll never find it. Do you know the Jordaan?'

'The Jor what?'

'Look I'm out of here in an hour. Shall I take you? There's just one thing about Pieter.'

'What?'

'I'll explain later,' she said.

I spent a restless hour waiting. What was it about Pieter that Jasmina wanted to tell me? I then have to confess I did something really girlie and uncool. I kept changing my clothes. My usual feelings of inadequacy took over. I wondered if this half brother of mine ever felt that too. I wanted to create a good impression. There was no one in the dorm, except Rixy. From time to time he looked up from one of his Goddam maps and watched me take off and try on everything I'd brought with me. Splayed over Miklos' bunk were several black jumpers. I crept past and grabbed one of the black roll necks and dashed out of the room, sure that Rixy like a hidden camera was watching my every move.

'You look really cool, Shaun,' Jasmina said, taking my arm as we wandered through the streets which became narrower and narrower. It

112

had an old toy town feel, which I didn't mention to Jasmina since we seemed back on equal, adult terms again.

Chapter 15

What happened next was such a jumbled, whirlwind of events that to start with I couldn't put them in any order at all. Don't you find that if you're really there, in the moment, you're too busy living it to think about it? Having lost my mobile I don't have any pictures of Pieter. That feels weird. It's as if I can't prove any of what happened next in Amsterdam.

I last left you, reader, with Jasmine and I walking the Jordaan. Between then and the ferry home it's no exaggeration to say that a whole lifetime of events has happened.

When Jaz, (she'd said I could call her Jaz which made me think she did actually like me), and I reached Pieter's flat I stood there, frozen in time. A really weird sensation went through my arm and I couldn't even send it a message to lift up my hand and press the buzzer. I could see Jaz watching me, with a kind of faraway look in her eyes as if she recognised my inability to move.

The heavy door swung open, behind it came a cool looking guy: jeans and leather jacket. Competition for Miklos, I thought. Jaz couldn't take her eyes off him. Alice stood behind him - my brother - and she was laughing her head off. She looked really relaxed, like I'd never seen her before.

'You took your time,' laughed Alice.

'Now we can finally get going!' said Piet.

This wasn't what I'd expected. In the movies you have these big emotional scenes. Instead, it was as if we'd always known each other.

We walked over little bridges, a world in miniature, to a tiny bar. The four of us. You know, I felt so happy at that moment. Nothing ever happened in my life. I was on some great adrenaline rush and never wanted to go back to Gt Waveney. I felt home, my life was here. We chatted just like a group of old friends. This time I declined the gin and found out how good Dutch beer is. After a few drinks the atmosphere changed. Jaz started asking Piet about his childhood. I wished she'd just shut up.

'Didn't you realise you were adopted?' she probed. 'After all, you don't look very Dutch?'

'That wasn't the only difference,' Piet explained. 'By four years old, disdain for them and everyone else started to show. I always knew I was adopted. I can't remember being told. Just that I was chosen. I climbed onto everything to distance myself. At age six I climbed onto the rooftops and tried to reach the clouds.'

'That's just so romantic,' said Jaz, gazing at him.

'It was when I was six and we went away with Dad on business that the differences showed up. Or, rather people were only too keen to point them out. He worked for De Vere's,' Jasmina and Alice's eyes lit up.

'Shaun, it's a diamond company. You must have been round a diamond factory. All the tourists do,' said Jaz. Alice and I shook our heads. Tassy and Dave would never do something so touristy. It was more the cringing kind of behaviour Mum and Dad would take part in, I thought.

'They're a girl's best friend,' laughed Alice.

'So we went to South Africa. I still remember the botanic gardens and going up Table Mountain in a cable car. Everywhere was bright, colourful. So different to the days of cold and fog in Holland in the winter. Yet, everyone else ruined it!' He slammed down his beer. The three of us seemed to shudder in unison. 'Apartheid was officially over, yet it takes more than laws to change people's attitudes. People stared at us in the street. I heard people say, 'What are they doing with a coloured boy?''

'Madonna, Angelina Jolie, they all adopt black children,' said Alice with a frown.

'I'm talking about fifteen years ago. People take time to catch up,' said Piet, a little calmed by Alice's comment.

'Later I found out that there'd been rumours back home that I was Dad's child with one of the coloured women in South Africa. He'd made so many trips out there. I never asked where my natural parents were from. I preferred to fantasise - create new identities for myself. One day a Spanish matador fighting bravely fighting bulls, or an Indian Maharajah on his throne, or a native American with my bow and arrow.' He moved his body as he talked and for a moment I really believed he was these people. 'It was the beginning of my wonderful career.'

'Some days I thought I was Indonesian. It was very cool in the eighties; you saw many mixed marriages of Dutch and Indonesian.' He laughed. We laughed too. And the tension, like a smoke screen lifted for a bit.

'By the time I turned sixteen, I'd been expelled from five schools for practising the art of the pickpocket on my teachers. They were a bad few years.'

'How did you do that!' exclaimed Jaz, as he held her purse high in the air.

'It was in my inside pocket. Nobody mucks about with Jasmina Batica,' she shouted. It's a bit embarrassing to admit this, but the look on her face and the way she shouted made me scared.

'It was when I was sixteen that Mum said she thought my real dad was from Iran. And my mother wasn't Dutch but English. It was their parting gift before retiring to South Africa. They invited me to go along. But I figured that South Africa wasn't ready for the likes of Piet Kostler.'
What was strange about him was this way of talking about himself, almost as if he were talking about a friend or relative of his.

'I guess I went a bit wild then. I made my living down on the Leidesplein doing magic. I lived on the edge of society. It wasn't long before the bars and clubs wanted me inside. I was taking all their punters. Soon I was invited to private parties and met a whole load of celebrities. Yet it wasn't enough. I think that was what drove me into the Big Brother house.' Jaz nudged me, as if to say I told you so.

'I was your B list celebrity all alone in the world.' This was hard to believe. Then he went on to tell us what it was like being adopted. Until then, even reading Mum's diary, I'd never thought much about adoption. If the truth was known, I'd often dreamed that my parent's weren't my own and there had been some great mistake and I'd ended up with Samantha and Keith through no fault of my own; whilst my real parents were off doing something really exciting or important to save the world. He must have read my thoughts.

'I've got friends say they wish they had different parents. None of them mean it. Not really. For family isn't just your parents - it's brothers, sisters, grandparents - the lot. When I got older and was no longer the cute kid, but instead the stroppy teenager, they all began to keep their distance - to disown me. Everyone that is, except Granddad. I thought his interest in me was because he really loved me, but his motives turned out to be far more complex than that.

'I channelled all my energy into the performance arts. Now I had this overwhelming urge to be seen, to prove myself. I really believed that the more that loved me the more loved I'd be. Fame was the spur,' said Piet. He had this odd, theatrical way of speaking which was like he was playing a part, reading someone's lines. In fact it seemed as if he spoke in a one man play, where he took all the parts.

'Tell us about the Big Brother house,' I asked.

'I was on track to win. Each week I prepared a new act to lure the voters. I'd become a household name in the Netherlands. There were a handful of us left. Yet it was that girl - Katrin, who ruined it all for me. She ruined everything.' Jaz was nodding, understanding something that I'd clearly missed. What I hadn't missed was that Piet finally seemed to be himself, playing the part of himself.

'What happened, Piet?' asked Alice, speaking my thoughts.

'It wasn't until I was evicted that I had any idea what had happened to me in that house. Katrin wasn't awful or anything. It was just the fact that she was going to give birth in the house.'

I nearly choked on my beer.

'That's gross,' I said.

'Got a problem with women, have you, Shaun?' said Jaz.

'I didn't have a problem with this Katrin having the baby. Or so I thought,' continued Piet. I was jealous that I couldn't do any trick that week which would surpass - a birth. But it wasn't until I sat in my flat feeling absolutely rotten and tired, just so tired that I realised what had bugged me. What had literally sent me mad? It was seeing her so close, so connected with this baby - I couldn't believe or understand how my mother had given me away.' He locked me in a steely stare and to be honest I just wished I could have disappeared into the ground there and then.

'Endless e-mails rolled in. Some kind, some really mean. I became a hermit. I'd never spent much time thinking. I'd always been hyper. Some kids like me get dosed up on drugs to calm them down. I'd channelled my energies into performing. Often only sleeping a few hours a night. The only visitor I allowed in was Granddad. It was when I was in hospital that Granddad visited and said it was time to tell me about my past. He dropped a bombshell. I'm a diamond baby. My dad paid your mum with a diamond. She sold me. That's why I wanted to see you. To tell you this. Let you know what your mother, she's not my mother, is really like!

'No. No. Mum would never do that.' I said on autopilot. 'We live in a little terraced house and when Dad was out of work we even got benefits. You're lying. You're like all those Big Brother people trying to make up stories to cause a scene.'

'Shaun I think he's telling the truth,' said Alice. I felt that awful feeling welling up again, like the time in the café.

Then you have to believe me, I'm not an aggressive type. I've usually run away from fights in the playground but this kind of rage happened before I could think about it. I'd hit Piet and of course he'd struck back. Before I knew it the barmen had us both out of the pub in the freezing cold.

'You're a f***in' liar. What are you playing at?' I yelled.

'Shaun, look I'll tell you all I remember. Dad gave Granddad a diamond to take to Gt Waveney. To buy me. It wasn't some great one, but worth a few thousand euros, enough to do something with back then, twenty years ago. There was some woman who'd put Granddad in touch with your mum.'

'What woman?'

'Oh, I don't remember. In fact I probably never knew. Granddad was a flower van driver, so I guess it would be a flower shop owner or maybe a market stall.'

'Mrs. Plumb,' I yelled.

'What?'

I suddenly remembered snippets from Mum's diary. Something had been given to Mrs. Plumb, not Mum.

'Piet,' I yelled. 'I can prove it to you. I can prove that our mum is okay.'

I unzipped my pocket and took out the little book. I felt well stressed thumbing through the pages trying to find the right bit. I could feel sweat dripping onto the pages.

'I've got it.' I yelled triumphantly.

'Read it to me,' commanded Piet.

I don't normally read out loud to anyone, but felt it wasn't the time to refuse.

'*The heavy doors clanked open. She pushed me into the giant refrigerator. The heavy door stood ajar, through the gap I saw him give her a tiny box, her eyes lit up as she opened it.*'

'*A girl's best friend!*' *she exclaimed.*

'*You know, several hundred years ago I could have given you one of these,*' *said the man, holding up a red tulip. 'They cost the price of a house!*'

'*Well I never. The likes of me would have been rich,*' *she said looking at the tulip delivery. 'Well I've got my own fortune now,*' *she winked. 'A florist shop, or maybe a cafe where I could serve up cream teas and black forest gateaux,*' *she said, licking her lips.*'

'It all makes sense now. Mum hates her and had a real fit when I started working there. But she never said why,' I said. The four of us all stood with tears streaming down our faces.

Chapter 16

When I stepped back on the ferry, the bar and the cabins looked familiar. I couldn't quite believe all that had happened in less than a week. Time had speeded up. My past, present and future had changed, been rewritten. I struggled to hold on to the order of events. There were lots of little gaps which needed to be filled in. One was what happened to Alice after she ran out on me at the American café.

Alice and I huddled in the corner of the ferry bar; some cheesy Hawaiian band played tunes which all merged into one. Then, coincidence of coincidences, Dave stepped into the bar in his own Hawaiian shirt. I think he blushed under his beard and marched out again, before he could see Alice and me breaking our curfew.

It was past midnight when the band finally packed up and Alice began to tell me all the details of what happened after she ran out on me at the American café.

'I stopped at the first internet café I found and Googled Piet Kostler. Of course I found the same site as you had. He looked really freaky with all those sequins stuck on his eyes and lips. I sat and stared at the computer. His long face and dark curly hair. The screen became a mirror. It was just like looking at a male version of me. He doesn't really look anything like you, Shaun, does he?'

It was true that Pieter didn't look much like me or Mum. It was the other things. I noticed the little things: the details. We all have this lop sided sort of grin that people mistake for a smirk.

'Then I sent an e-mail and got the same odd auto reply as you had. I didn't write a letter. I guess I've got a bit of an issue with doing what I'm told! He was well out of order trying to boss me around.'

I really envied Alice's way of not being bossed around. I'm too eager to please everyone.

'Instead I scribbled down the address and ran out of the internet café,' she said. 'My impatience got the better of me. I hailed a taxi, rehearsing what I was going to say to Piet, and went straight to the Jordaan district. The lights were all out. I rang on the bell and nothing, no answer. I waited and waited on the doorstep. I even vowed to sit on the step all night if necessary. Luckily, that didn't happen. When I saw his face on the web site I thought how handsome he was. I sat on the doorstep I'd played out little scenarios about introducing him to Dotty and the others. How they would all squabble over him. Even Miklos would be put in his place.'

'You don't fancy Miklos?'

'Of course not. He's just a show off. I was winding him up, and maybe you, too,' she laughed. 'The old streets were deserted. Silent. Then the footsteps. I don't know how to say this, Shaun. I was disappointed. I think I must be a really awful person to say it. I hadn't expected him to arrive in costume - his face painted blue and wearing a frilly dress!'

'You wanted him to be normal, you mean.'

She nodded. 'I felt a real fraud too. I'm supposed to be an art student. Yet seeing him dressed as a work of art.....'Yeah, I'd have preferred jeans and a leather jacket,' she confessed.

Nothing much else happened on the way back to Gt Waveney - well to me at least. Silently we walked through 'nothing to declare'. We trudged along through the empty walkway. From nowhere sprang the customs officers. Tassy and Dave were the first to be stopped. We all laughed, thinking it was some kind of joke. The joke stopped when they took Alice aside.

'Are you with her?' asked the silver haired customs man. He didn't look like a customs officer. His hair reminded me of a male hairdresser, so foolishly, as it happened, I nodded.

I felt a curious mix of fear and excitement when they searched through every last thing in Alice's bag: the paint palettes, tampons - the lot! We finally saw the light of day, only to see Miki and Nikki being searched.

'Always do it to us, they do! Racist bastards!' yelled Nikki.

To be honest I'd never thought much about racism until I saw Alice and the twins being picked out from our group. It sent a chill down my spine and reminded me of those old Second World War films, the Nazis in their swanky uniforms choosing the Jews and gypsies for the death camps. If there's a thing I really hate it's people judging you by what you look like, or what it says about you on a piece of paper. It made me think of my school statement which followed me around, saying I couldn't read and write. The thing was everyone thought I was stupid. Not being able to read and write well isn't a judge of intelligence. Just as having a foreign name or looks doesn't mean you're a terrorist or drug trafficker. It just made me so mad. So powerless.

Chapter 17

Back home life carried on. In many ways it carried on as normal. Normal is what I call my pre-Amsterdam life. I hadn't expected that to happen. Mum became even more distant going off swimming at odd times of the day and night. In a way I was glad that Dad was off-shore for those few weeks, for I'd have ended up telling him about Piet and the trip. I'm not good at secrets. Words just seem to stream out before I've thought about it. Other people's secrets are another thing. I hate being shut out, in the dark.

I'd actually had to persuade Piet to communicate with us by e-mail; not that silly old letter writing stuff. For one thing he wouldn't have been able to read anything I sent and secondly I wouldn't be able to read what he and Mum were talking about. I couldn't help reading Mum's e-mails.

From: Samantha Colby,scolby@hotmail.co.uk
To: <piet1@versanet.nl>
Date: Sunday, November 21, 2006 11.45PM
Subject: Old friends

Dear Piet,
Thanks for the e-mail and the latest photos. I finally managed to open them with a little help from Shaun. I've, or should I say Shaun, has attached some golden oldies for you - don't laugh when you look at them. I've borrowed these off Jonathan, an old friend.

LOST FOR WORDS

I'm ever so pleased that you want us to meet - and so nervous just in case you are disappointed in me. Keith doesn't know yet, as I said, I'm playing that one by ear. I'll know when the moment is right to tell him. Please do come and visit though, I'll sort out this end; you're more than welcome anytime. Phone me at work and we can make some arrangements, my number is 01493 6000586 ext 58, but just ask for me, my hours are 8.30 - 4.30. Although I guess there is an hour's time difference. I will be on holiday for a few days from 11th December - to do some Christmas shopping.

This past month has been a very emotional time for me. I don't know if you can understand, but when I decided to have you adopted I had to lock it away in my mind otherwise I wouldn't have been able to cope with it. I'm not saying you weren't ever thought about because that wouldn't be true - every so often something would remind me.

Then when Shaun found you it was like going back twenty years and at times full of 'if only' or 'if I'd done this or that'. A lot of guilt wondering if you felt bitter against me. Having read your e-mails though and looked at your photos and seeing what a handsome man you are, I feel so proud of you and your parents and family because they have brought you up to be the man you are.

When I left school I wanted to do something to do with art and design - anything. But I went into a shop, doing window design. Then a lot of shops closed down here and I managed to get in an advertising agency. I was on reception, typing etc. I remember I fell in love with a boy in the art department there. He was ever so shy and we used to gaze at each other when I walked past his window. I enjoyed it there, but when I found out I was pregnant (well about five months after) instead of telling them, which I couldn't face I just upped and left without any explanation. It was around that time Dad died. My Dad had been a fisherman and his dad before that. He'd been ill for some time with lymphoma, a blood disease. I stayed at home with my Mum, who was devastated by Dad's death and then to find out I was pregnant - she just gave up. Now I know it was a nervous breakdown. I stayed in the house for a bit, and then I went to Amsterdam where I had you. After that I didn't want to stay in Gt Waveney and went to London. The next episode to follow!

We were all upset at the weekend as we had to have the cat put down. She'd been ill for a long time but I had to make the decision and it was heartbreaking, Picasso was like one of the family.

Anyway I had better close instead of rambling on. Wait for you to phone!

Kind regards
Samantha

Chapter 18

The main difference in my life, apart from seeing Alice, was quitting the bakery. I'd seriously thought of carrying on working there; after all I needed the money and nowhere else would employ someone as numerically dysfunctional as me. It was Nan who'd come up with a way out. In fact she became my main backer or investor. She complained that she was too old to still be working and wanted some time to enjoy herself. She gave me some money for the ingredients and her old pans from the bed and breakfast (I forgot to add that I ruined all Mum's saucepans with my initial experiments). Nan wasn't all sweetness and light, she was quite a businesswoman and insisted on a 10% cut on my profits. I wasn't in a position to argue or complain.

Heating up the sugar to the right temperature was hard at first. Then I remembered this really mad TV chef who worked like a scientist in a lab. I felt like him, a mad professor spending hours making caramelized slabs, cracking the mixture, spinning sugar. My sugar city became my college and my home project. I have to admit I became obsessed with it.

Of course, the tutors wanted research, drawings, and plans of what I was going to make. I didn't work like that. My one concession to research was a trip to the candyfloss stall. I'd spent my whole life buying candyfloss, always entranced as the sugar spun round. It was always the same shape, no-one ever made exciting forms: pyramids, cones, turrets. After a few mouthfuls I threw the disgusting cotton-wool-tasting concoction in the bin.

Unlike the boring candyfloss mound, I wanted to explore all possibilities. How would I know what worked and what didn't until I started making them? It's hard to explain, but when I'm designing I can see the shape of my sugar buildings in my mind. It was harder to translate that into a drawing. And I didn't want to waste time trying. So I thanked God for the digital camera. Like the Big Brother show I recorded every step of my experiments for the college's precious evidence.

By December I had a whole sugar city in miniature. Some were sugar-crafted pieces like the wedding cakes. But what I loved most were the semi transparent buildings in a rich caramel glaze.

LOST FOR WORDS

Sam's story

Sam Andersen held out her miniature video camera and moved around the market. She was almost unrecognizable in her black trousers and black coat. She talked into a mouthpiece, every so often saying nothing and picking up the voices of market traders and their customers.

Mrs. Plumb inhaled the crisp, sea air as she set out across the market. A thick layer of frost purified the market square. The canvas stall tops sparkled in their mid-winter camouflage. The big chill was forecast to stay and so the yellow and red stripes would lay dormant until the New Year. From behind the pound stall she watched Dennis serve his customers. Twice a week he stood flanked by pastel coloured knickers, which swayed like flags in the wind. A wind had blown in straight from Siberia. Or so her family had always said.

She headed towards Dennis Colby's stall. She picked up several pairs and put them down again. None of them seemed quite right. Finally, she lingered over some flesh-coloured big knickers. She ran her hand across the satin fabric, caressing it as if a loved one.

'Shall I see if we've got your size?' inquired Mr. Colby. 'These are selling like hot cakes. Husbands, boyfriends, you name it. My busiest day of the year so far.'

'Two pairs please. If you've got them.'

The knickers were Mrs. Plumb's annual treat. Her Christmas present to herself. She said Jonathan and Mr. Plumb never bought her nought.

Mrs. Plumb carried the dainty black and gold striped bag across the market to the chip van. Like beacons, the steaming chimneys of the chippy drew in the cold and hungry. She heard the clock chime twelve.

'Where is he?' Mrs. Plumb gobbled down a cone of piping hot chips.

'Sorry, Mum. Couldn't find anywhere to park. Gt Waveney never used to be so busy!' exclaimed Jonathan.

'It's all those second home-owners down the coast,' she splattered through her chips.

'How about I treat you to a pint of cockles? They always were your favourite, Mum.'

They were about to head off to the cockle stall when Mrs. Plumb stopped and saw the long queue at the stall in the corner. Sam hid behind the flapping canvas of the pound stall.

Mrs. Plumb bustled over to the cake stall, never one to miss a bargain. The sugar city was arranged like a scene from Santa's Grotto.

'So this is where all my regulars have come, all my Christmas orders,' exclaimed Glynis Plumb. It hadn't half been quiet for the time of year at the Upper Crust. 'Tell you what. I'll throw one of these houses in as well,' said Alice, always keen to keep the peace.

'Those darkies, Bosnians, Poles, Portuguese, taking all my customers,' she complained holding onto Jonathan's arm. 'But at least I've got you home - at last,' she said squeezing his black cashmere coat. 'Jonathan, you've gone as white as those there chalets.'

He shook her hand off him and walked round to the back of the cake stall. He stared at Alice. It wasn't the dark eyes, or the shape of her full mouth, but that smile. Jonathan saw Darius' wide grin as she handed the old lady her change for the Christmas cake. A cold gush of wind slapped his face.

Then the penny dropped.

'I know, well, knew, your dad. For a while we were best friends.'

'My Dad. Darius Nazemi,' said the girl stacking up a fresh supply of goods. Jonathan and Alice were huddled together deep in conversation, when they heard a commotion at the other end of the stall.

'My God, it's him - Shaun,' screamed Mrs. Plumb. 'You little liar, after all I've done for that scumbag family of yours. She turned to Jonathan. 'He told me he had too much college work, now look at him serving up the cakes. Don't you go buying anything off those there Andersens.'

Jonathan pulled a card out of his pocket and pressed it into Shaun's hand, just before his mother pulled him, like a toddler, away from the sweetie stall.

'We won't let that get in the way of our Christmas. Your first Christmas here for years. I can picture Christmas Day: the turkey sizzling in the oven, the Brussels on the boil. Then, after lunch you and I can sit together on the sofa and watch the Queen's speech.'

Sam tapped Jonathan on the arm. He swung round and looked straight through her, noting something familiar, yet not quite sure who she was.

'I didn't recognise you at first,' he grinned. You look so different. 'So young.' Sam blushed. 'What's all this,' he said pointing to her camera.

'I'm an art student now - well part-time. Too soon to give up the day job.' He moved closer, put his hand on her shoulder and whispered into her ear, glancing over to the cake stall.

'No need to whisper,' said Sam. 'I don't have any secrets anymore,' she said, loud enough for Mrs. Plumb to hear loud and clear over the bustle of the market traders.

Chapter 19

I have to confess that what happened to me at the market was nothing short of a miracle. You'll think it sounds like one of those stories where top models are talent spotted whilst walking around Debenhams. Unless of course you believe that we create our own luck.

This old guy came over to the cake stall. He looked really carefully at the sugar city; then looked up at my hand painted price board and began to chuckle. He started asking me these really interesting questions.

'How do you think up the shapes for the buildings?'

'I see it all in my head, without the need for any drawings,' I said. He kept nodding. 'I feel uncomfortable and frustrated until I get it absolutely right. If it's half a millimeter out it seems like two metres to me.' I'd never talked to anyone like that before. There was something so comforting about the way he absolutely understood what I was saying. I'd never talked like that to anyone about my work before. He looked around the market,

'I love these spaces where you can just let the world go by. In fact in my line of work I concentrate best when I'm surrounded by people.'

'What do you do?' I asked, not really expecting someone of his age to still be working.

'I'm an architect.'

'I've never met an architect before,' I said. I felt my heart race. I was really excited. 'I didn't think there were any architects in Gt Waveney!' I blurted.

'Well, I'm the first! I don't live round here, though. We're just renting the lighthouse down at Dunstowe for the Christmas holidays.' I should have guessed as much, for his soft, expensive lemon-coloured jumper stood out a mile in Gt Waveney. We carried on chatting for I don't know how long. Then it happened. He handed me a business card. It was my first encounter with a hero, a real celebrity, at least in my eyes. Here stood the man behind so many of the great, modern buildings I'd just seen in books or on television. Then to add the icing on the cake, sorry, I couldn't resist the pun, he said:

'Would you like to be an intern at our architectural partnership?'

'Yes! Yes!' I said unable to conceal my enthusiasm and a little scared to ask exactly what an internship was.

He stopped for a moment and bit into one of my houses. 'Or maybe you should come and train at my wife's restaurant. I think you'll find we have a lot in common: buildings, food....' he then pointed to my price board. 'And this too. Just during the holidays until you've finished your course.'

'The prices,' I said, looking at the board. 'Do you think I'm asking over the odds?'

'No,' he said, 'you're selling them a little too cheaply, if I may say so. It wasn't the prices which caught my attention. It was the idea of eating the slimiest house in the world!'

'What. It's the slimmest house,' I said.

'Well, of course that's what you meant. But it's not what you wrote. Is it? You see I should know. I'll let you into a secret. I may have received a knighthood and designed some of the greatest buildings of the twentieth century...'

'The Pompidou Centre, Madrid Airport....' I filled in the answers.

'Yet I was sent to a school for backward children and barely ever passed an exam. In many ways my dyslexia has been the making of me. It stands to reason that if the system doesn't work for you, you try to redesign it.'

I nodded unable to believe this conversation was really taking place.

'You come to me for an intern and the world's your oyster: the Royal College of Art wouldn't turn its doors on such talent. After all, did you know that a quarter of their students are dyslexic?'

With that he vanished, as quickly as if he were a wizard.

So there it is your happy ending. All my dreams came true. A chance to work for the top British architect, a newly found brother and a kind of girlfriend. But that wasn't quite the end. Piet's New Year visit to Gt Waveney took an unexpected course of events.

Chapter 20

My next project was to record the New Year's Day swim. I charged up the video, not quite able to believe that making a film could really be homework. After Amsterdam I began to notice all sorts of little details about Gt Waveney. I guess I'd just thought everywhere was a bit like Gt Waveney, probably because I'd never really been anywhere else. Everyone who was anyone would be at the swim. It would make an ideal snapshot of life there, I thought. And not forgetting that after endless letters and e-mails Piet had arrived in Gt Waveney.

Alice and I joined Dad and Nan on the cliff top. From the headland the snaking line of the procession formed into a semi-circle around its leader. The old man, the priest, was dressed in black from head to toe. The crowd, indistinguishable dots, like pixels on a screen, moved back as he lifted up his arm. Out from his darkness, like a wizard appeared not a wand but a silver cross. It glistened in the metallic blue of the winter light and reminded me of a sword. Except the sunlight cheapened its appearance, as if it was some prize from the amusement arcade. He proudly flung the cross into the sea.

'Hurrah!' They cheered. The cross bobbed about for a moment, and then was gone.

From the jetty, pale torsos hit the icy water.

'They're like Lucien Freud's paintings. So fleshy and pink,' said Alice, her sketchbook flapping about in the breeze. Their day-glow swimwear, marked them out against the grey water. Mum wasn't so daft - in her super duper new 'skin' wetsuit. Piet, on the other hand was dressed up in his full carnival regalia.

'He doesn't feel the cold when he goes in. That one there. He swims in the sea all year round,' said Dad, trying to sound an expert on the swim. Alice grasped my hand and I nodded, unsure as to whether Dad was talking to us in particular, or to himself.

'Best get down to give Piet his hot chocolate and sympathy,' I said, pulling Alice away from Dad and Nan.

'He'll have the North Sea in his bones now, like his Granddad,' croaked Nan, 'he won't be out yet.'

'They won't manage in there much longer. Another five minutes and we'll have the lifeboat out. They've usually got it by now,' said Dad, nestled in his parka and scarf. 'I'll follow you down with your mum's refreshments,' he said.

Down by the jetty, one by one the shivering swimmers emerged. Their flesh, now the grey-blue colour of the water. I zoomed in on the goose bumps and drops of salt water.

Miki wrapped Nikki in towels and force-fed him piping hot chocolate. I managed to get a full Niki Mavroudis in distress expression - he'll kill me for it! The local TV crew moved away from the crowd and silently packed away their equipment.

'No good luck this year then,' said Tony Mavroudis, still in dark glasses.

'I've had mine this year,' I whispered into Alice's ear.

'We've had ours. Our family's reunited,' whispered Mum, squeezing Dad's hand, whilst he wrapped her in towels.

'You know it's our tradition that the one who reaches the cross first is recognised as the godfather of Jesus.'

"Um," said Mum and Dad in happy unison. For once Dad wasn't cowering to Tony. In fact I'd have to say Tony looked a bit jealous.

'You get a year long blessing,' said Tony.

'Where's Piet?' shouted Alice. 'The others are all out now.' Her face turned as cold as the New Year's Day.

'Look!' I shouted. 'It's him.' Bobbing up and down against the waves were Piet's sequins and feathers. Mum ran back along the jetty and dived in, like some proper athlete. She dragged Piet along; he was carrying the cross in his teeth. They clambered on to the jetty only to collapse into Dad's arms. Jonathan Plumb ran along in his shiny black shoes, dressed for the City not the sea and stuffed glucose and Mars bars into Piet.

'Keep talking! Look he's passing out,' screamed Alice.

My film was snapped up by the news companies.

'More fool them. Fancy leaving before the real action began,' Nan had said. 'And I hope they're paying you for it.' I wasn't interested in the money. Mum and Piet being okay, and my film work appearing on national telly was enough for me.

Chapter 21

From: Samantha Colby,scolby@hotmail.co.uk
To: <piet1@versanet.nl>
Date: Saturday, January 6, 2007 9.45PM
Subject: The visit

Dear Piet,

Hope you have recovered from your visit to us! How did you get on with your flat hunting? Amsterdam sounds worse than London on that front. I kept thinking of you on Wednesday and hoped that you'd get one. Jasmina sounds a very interesting girl and I'd love to meet her soon.

I don't know what your feelings are but I loved the visit and so did Shaun and Keith. I hope it wasn't too traumatic for you, the New Year swim excluded! On our part it seemed so natural and easy. Shaun and Keith said they felt as if they'd known you for years, and my Mum thinks you're lovely.

Guess what, Mum's boyfriend has proposed! He's a fast worker, she's only known him just over a week. The doctor sent her to a dyslexic in the older person meeting. That was where they met. She said no, by the way. Apparently he was going too fast for her. Like I said to her though, at his age he can't go in for long courtships! Whether she will marry him or not I don't know, she keeps insisting he's too old for her.

My boss was very good when I went in on Wednesday. He said he wasn't going to ask me any questions as long as I was okay. Which was just as well as I hadn't got any answers for him. And of course you're a celebrity here, front page of the Gt Waveney Mercury, 'Our cousin from across the North Sea finds the Cross.' I've scanned it, all myself without any help, as an attachment and hope you can open it.

I hope your Mum and Dad haven't been too upset. I'm glad the presents will come in useful for the new flat. The Christmas parcels weren't meant to try and buy you. I know I never can or would want to do that. And the lost years can't be made up for. You know that I met your Mum all those years ago and she was a lovely lady. Although I can understand that she doesn't want to meet - at the moment. Maybe it's for the best for now that they are in South Africa

The painter turned up on Monday and he's painted the outside of the house. It looks nice. DIY was never Keith's strong point.

On Thursday night I think everything hit me - not just the past few months but the past almost twenty-one years. I'm so sorry that Darius is dead, yet having Alice tell you about him is a bonus I never imagined when I first asked Shaun to find you. I can't write about it now as its too painful, but I can just tell you that you were loved, still are, and it was the hardest thing I've ever done to have you adopted and to have all of us sat round a table after that swim, no one can imagine what that meant to me.

Must close now - it's very late. I'm home alone, Keith is on the rigs and Shaun is staying with Alice in London for a few days.

Love
Samantha

LOST FOR WORDS

From: Samantha Colby,scolby@hotmail.co.uk
To: <piet1@versanet.nl>
Date: Sunday, November 20, 2007 10.30PM
Subject: hello

Dear Piet,

Thanks for your letter. It's so nice to receive a letter in this age of e-mails. It really cheered me up, I had been feeling really fed up for some reason. I enjoyed my weekend in Amsterdam too. As you say we do seem to get on better each time we meet, which is good. I had to travel back to Heathrow. They were looking for people to switch from the Norwich flight. I didn't do badly, I got £200 and a taxi to my door.

Do you realise it was exactly a year ago this weekend that Shaun phoned me from Amsterdam to say that he had found you? It's been a very emotional year for us both, and Shaun too, of course, but I hope the start of an understanding and a friendship which will go on. On my part I can't tell you how happy it's made me, it's something I had thought about and hoped but sometimes still can't believe it. Do you remember me telling you about the astrologer and that my job would change in the autumn? Well it has. I've left work and am now at college full-time. I put it down to my trip and realising how fast time goes. They've been very flexible letting me change about part way through the term. Keith says they just want my money! My photography course was just the start of things. He came up from Brighton to help me choose suitable college clothes. He's all settled there, unable to move away from the sea, and it's the best architecture course in the country. He says he's going to build a house-boat and sail over to Holland - so watch this space. He's very busy working a day a week for that architect he met in Gt Waveney. He says one day a week in London is enough for him.

He promises that he'll write to you, but as you know writing's not his strong point.

Well, must close now, hope to see you soon. Don't worry about the fare if you and Jasmina want to come over. I'll see to that.

Write soon
Love Samantha.

Printed in the United Kingdom
by Lightning Source UK Ltd.
135449UK00001B/107/P